SURROGATES

K D GRACE

mischief

Mischief
An imprint of HarperCollins*Publishers*
77–85 Fulham Palace Road,
Hammersmith, London W6 8JB

www.mischiefbooks.com

A Paperback Original 2013

First published in Great Britain in ebook format by
HarperCollins*Publishers* 2012

Copyright © K D Grace 2012

K D Grace asserts the moral right to
be identified as the author of this work

A catalogue record for this book is
available from the British Library

ISBN-13: 9780007534760

Set in Sabon by FMG using Atomik ePublisher from Easypress

Find out more about HarperCollins and the environment at
www.harpercollins.co.uk/green

CONTENTS

Chapter One

'Francie? Francie, are you there?'

Dan made his way around behind the jungle of runner beans, getting a shoeful of soil when he stepped off the path. As the warm, moist earth infiltrated his dress socks, he would have cursed his clumsiness, but then he saw her on hands and knees, the swell of her hips slightly raised in her efforts to pull stubborn weeds. She didn't have to do that. She was the head kitchen gardener, a goddess in her domain. He hired underlings to do the weeding, but fuck, he was glad she took the hands-on approach, especially at times like this. She had kicked off the silly blue plastic gardening clogs she always wore, and her bare toes curled into the soft earth as though the very touch of it was an irresistible pleasure. How could soil between toes be so goddamned sexy?

The thin summer skirt she wore barely covered the heart-shaped roundness of her bottom, hugging her and clinging in the heavy summer heat to the delicious juncture where her thighs met. There were clearly no panty lines. She gardened in skirts, like she wanted to expose herself, like the acts of planting and digging and cultivating made her a naughty bitch who couldn't get enough. But then that was the way he saw her in his fantasies, and oh shit, did he have fantasies about her! His cock jerked with an insistence that nearly took his breath away. 'There you are,' he breathed, fingers already fumbling at his fly.

'Go away. I'm busy,' she said, giving some unfortunate weed an angry tug, an act that made the thin skirt quiver, made the firm muscles of her buttocks beneath clench and release. And his balls surged, sending a testosterone buzz clear to the crown of his head.

He ignored the anger in her voice. Well, he didn't actually ignore it. Her saucy temper made his cock even harder. 'It's all right, darling, you keep on working. Just lift your skirt for me.' He grunted softly as he released his cock into his hand.

'Lift it yourself. I said I'm busy.'

'You know I can't do that, sweetheart.'

She growled something particularly feral under her

breath. He figured it wasn't fit for polite company, which made him wish all the more that he'd heard it.

'I've got such a load for you. I'll come all over it if you don't lift it for me,' he said.

'I have other skirts, Daniel.' She only called him Daniel when she was really angry. 'Why do I care where you come?'

'Because you know where I really want to come, darling, and you have to know how badly I want it.' He moved slightly to one side, not so far that her magnificent bottom wasn't the centre of his attention, but far enough that, in her peripheral vision, she might catch a glimpse of him stroking his cock. Even if she couldn't, she knew what he was doing, and he had no intention of being quiet about it. He lifted his balls free from his boxers and groaned at the feel of himself, so full, so heavy for her.

She gave another angry yank at the offending weeds, and the resulting squeeze of her buttocks nearly sent him over the edge.

He spat on his hand noisily, rubbed his saliva over the length of his cock and groaned again, squinting at her exquisite backside as though if he just stared at it hard enough he could slide the skirt up over her hips with sheer desire. And the view would be magnificent. The way her knees were open, the way she braced herself on the garden mat, would showcase the tight dark bud of her anus nestled just above the splayed pout of her pussy. And her pussy, he had no doubt, would be slickened from knowing what he was doing, from knowing what he'd come for, what he so desperately wanted … needed.

'You were with her, weren't you? You were with your wife,' she said, reaching a gloved hand to deposit a handful of weeds in the trug next to her, an act that made the skirt ride up even further, leaving him breathless.

'What? No! I wasn't. I promise. I had a meeting with my accountant that overran. I swear it, Francie darling. I haven't seen Bel since I got home. Besides she's staying over at her sister's this evening. They're having a girls' night out. Sweetheart, you know if I were with her, I'd tell you. Haven't I always been above board about what goes on between Bel and me?'

She knew he had. Not that there was much to tell, but on the odd occasion when Bel had had too much wine with dinner and demanded he do his husbandly duty, or when she was feeling morose about her advancing years, all thirty-four of them, and needed to be shown she was still sexy, he never lied about it. It didn't matter what sex acts he'd had to perform to please his wife; when Francie asked for details, he gave them. A part of him hated that she always asked. Surely she knew it would be easier if she didn't know, but she couldn't seem to help herself. And he didn't hold back anything, even though he was always careful to remind her that, when he did his duty where Bel was concerned, it was thinking about her, Francie, that made him come.

And all the while he told Francie what he'd done to Bel, told her details that made him blush, details that made his cock stretch and arch towards her, she listened while her cunt got slick and fat. Even as those details made her angry and unhappy, she asked for them. And while he told her, she played with herself, fingers darting furiously in and out between her heavy slippery folds, hips shifting and grinding as she asked him in clipped, breathless words for more details. What did Bel's pussy look like? How did she smell? Could he taste the wine she'd drunk or the spices from Cook's curry when he ate her out? How hard did her nipples get? Did she talk dirty when he pushed into her? Jesus, having sex with Bel, even though he knew it hurt Francie, was almost worth it to watch the way Francie took the pain, twisted it, turned it, reshaped it and came on it, came in lovely gushing female squirts at what she had made of it in her filthy little head.

Of course she didn't like it that someone else got his cock while she only got to watch him wank. He didn't like it either, but there was nothing for it at the moment. As much as he wanted Francie, as much as he dreamed of riding her raw, he was still married to Bel, and he would stay faithful until he got the balls to ask for a divorce. No matter how badly he wanted Francie, he could never behave towards Bel the way his father had towards his mother.

So why was he such a coward? People got divorced every day. Lots of people. Hell, he knew people who had already been married and divorced multiple times. It was a simple thing to ask for a divorce these days. And yet here he was like a damned adolescent begging for a peek under a girl's skirt. 'Please, darling,' he said. 'I don't have a lot of time, and I want to spend what I do have with you.'

He saw the sigh shiver up through her body, and he knew he'd been forgiven. She knelt up enough to take off her gloves, then with one hand she eased the skirt up over her hips and wriggled slightly to open her legs a little wider on the mat.

He pressed his thumb to the head of his cock. The urge to come at the sight of her all engorged and open was nearly overwhelming. The pearlescent sheen on the inside of her pouting labia told him he wasn't the only one who needed to come. As she arched her back downward and forced her bottom even higher, her clit came into view looking like a heavy swollen marble at the apex of her pussy. 'Oh, Francie,' he breathed, 'touch it for me.'

She dipped her index and middle fingers in between her slick folds then drew them upward tightly against either side of her clit until it bulged still further, like soft, ripe fruit waiting to be nibbled. And, fuck, how he wished he could!

'Do you like that?' she murmured, glancing over her shoulder.

'Oh God, yes,' he grunted.

'I thought you weren't going to show. I was angry,' she said. 'Oh, I definitely had plans for the vegetables I was sending Cook for your dinner tonight.' She nodded at the basket of mixed phallic veg sitting on the ground next to her.

His cock jerked. 'Show me,' he whispered. 'Show me what you were going to do to my veg.'

She took a heavy courgette slightly thicker than his cock, crooked and arched nearly in the shape of a banana. She gave it a leisurely deep-throating that had him thumbing the underside of his cock again, that had him imagining how it would feel if it were him getting the benefit of her delicious tongue. Her cheek muscles tugged and pulled on the courgette like it was a rod of steel.

When she was absolutely certain she had his full attention, she repositioned herself to face him. She wriggled her bare arse down on to the mat with her legs splayed. With one hand she scrunched her skirt into a wad just below her navel, raking her long slender hand over tightly trimmed pubic curls, then she slid two fingers into her milky cunt and opened herself. With a little lifting of her buttocks and shifting of her hips she was ready. She snugged the hard jut of the courgette up tight against her reluctant pout.

Suddenly it was as though he weren't even there, and that made it all the harder for him to hold his wad. She spat on her fingers and rubbed saliva around the place where the courgette met the tight press of her cunt hole. As though the task at hand demanded all the focus in the world, she alternately lubricated and pushed, lubricated and pushed, all the while making tight little grunting sounds low in her belly. He couldn't take his eyes off the slow but relentless yielding of her grudging pussy to the press of the veg. With each push, with each shift, her clit marbled and beaded harder and harder just above the nudging of the courgette. She continued to push and stroke, push and stroke until at last her pussy hole yielded, her eyes fluttered and she caught her breath in a little gasp as the veg slid cock-deep into her gash.

'Ah!' she breathed. 'That's better. That's just what I needed. Such a tight fit, but oh so yummy.' Then she raised her eyes to meet his and offered him a smile that was almost shy. 'Now I'm ready to come.' Fingers still wet from her efforts with the veg, she undid the buttons of her sundress, releasing high firm breasts topped with heavy raspberry nipples into the pinching, kneading caress of one hand.

'I don't know about you –' she grunted as she began to thrust and gyrate against the veg '– but I won't be able to hold back long with all this heft up in my tight little fanny. And when I'm done coming, I'll let you take the veg to the house for Cook. That way if you want to sneak a taste of my cunt, who'll know?' With each breathless thrust she lifted her arse off the gardening mat, giving him teasing glimpses of her gripping anus, and she knew exactly what he was looking at. She offered a throaty chuckle. 'Maybe next time I'll let you watch me shove a nice plump carrot back there. You'd like that, wouldn't you?'

He only nodded. This was the point in their wank sessions where he always fell silent, too taken in by the heat of her, by the want of her, by the knowing that this was as much as he could allow himself of her, no matter how willing she was. He yanked at his cock like it was a wild thing he had to tame. He yanked until it hurt, and he kneaded his balls, feeling the surge at the base all ready to spill out on to the warm earth in front of Francie. It was the best he had to offer her right now, his humiliation, his need, his lust once removed.

She fell back on to the ground with a little cry, legs apart, offering him an exquisite view of the tremors of her orgasm tightly stretched around the courgette. The view, combined with the ripe scent of her, was more than he could endure, and he unloaded in heavy spurts on to the ground scant centimetres from her bare thigh. He unloaded till he thought he'd turn himself inside out, convulsing and grunting until he was spent, bent forward on his knees in the veg bed next to her, gasping and gulping for breath.

It was almost enough to give him the courage to ask Isabel for a divorce. He was sure he could almost do it after such erotic bliss, and what a lovely surprise it would be for Francie. But before he could verbalise that bliss, Bel's voice rang out over the garden wall.

'Dan? Dan, are you there?' Fortunately they heard her before she found them.

Francie cursed under her breath, grabbed the basket and fled into the greenhouse.

With a painful effort, Dan shoved his cock into his trousers and kicked at the earth to bury the evidence. 'Coming, Bel.' He fought hard not to sound breathless as his wife, dressed in tight jeans and a vest that showed plenty of her ample cleavage, stepped through the gate. He forced a smile. 'I thought you were at your sister's for the night, sweetheart.'

'We had to cancel. She's down with some sort of stomach virus.' She grimaced. 'God knows, I don't need that.' She took his arm. 'I'll be keeping you company this evening, darling. I thought maybe we'd make our own entertainment a little later. My massage therapist says sex is great for keeping the skin looking young. She says you'd be surprised at all the health benefits of an active sex life.'

Dan gave a quick glance over his shoulder, hoping desperately that Francie hadn't overheard, but she had disappeared.

Bel continued. 'Cook told me you were out here, so I thought I'd come down and have Francie send up a few more veg for dinner. During my massage today, Ellen also told me that we'd both benefit from eating more veg. She says a diet full of veg is the next best thing to the fountain of youth.' She gestured exuberantly. 'She says veg and sex are the keys to health and vitality. She says Francie probably grows most of the veggie super-foods right here in her garden.' She looked around. 'Where is Francie anyway? You haven't seen her, have you?

Chapter Two

'I must be out of my fucking mind.' Francie shoved the basket of vegetables that would enhance Dan and Bel's dinner tonight on to the big staging table in the greenhouse and wiped frantically at her eyes with the backs of her hands. She wasn't about to cry. She wouldn't give the bastard the satisfaction.

They were going to feast on her vegetables. Her vegetables would give them the strength and stamina to make their own entertainment. Wasn't that what Bel said? Make their own fucking entertainment, and why not? The woman was his wife. And Francie was nothing more than the hired help. The stupid hired help, who didn't have enough brains to stay away from her gorgeous boss! Make that her arsehole boss, she mentally corrected herself. She bit back a sob and grabbed a tray of basil seedlings from the incubator. Cook wanted a couple of new basil plants for the kitchen. Bel had it in her head that basil was the herb of eternal youth and had practically been grazing on the stuff recently.

'Excuse me, have you seen Dan?'

Francie spun around and nearly jumped out of her skin at the sight of the unexpected man standing so close behind her. She dropped the tray, and seedlings and compost exploded on to the floor.

That was it. That was the straw that broke the gardener's back. She'd babied those seedlings along for weeks now, keeping them safe and warm and trauma-free, then this happens. She burst into tears.

'Oh God! Oh God! I'm so sorry. I didn't mean to startle you. Please don't cry. Here, let me help you.'

But it was suddenly like the dam had burst. She had endured all these weeks of wanting Dan so badly, all these weeks of knowing that no matter what he said, no matter how hot their wank sessions were, at the end of the day it wasn't her bed he shared. Then there were all the weeks of feeling guilty because while he stayed faithful to Bel, she didn't care. She would have fucked him in a New York minute. And she liked Bel. That was a part of the problem. Bel was OK. Bel was wonderful. Still, she would have fucked him if he'd asked. But he didn't. And it all bubbled over in one upturned tray of basil seedlings.

13

'Here, sit down. Please don't cry. I'll take care of it,' the man was saying, guiding her away from the mess on the floor. 'There, there. It'll be OK. Basil seedlings are tough. They'll be OK, just please stop crying. Can I get you some water? Aspirin, maybe? Anything?' He didn't wait for her to answer. Instead he guided her to the stool near the staging table and settled her gently on to it. Then he knelt, scooped the spilled compost into the tray and began to replant the seedlings one by one. 'There, you see? It'll be OK. You see, no damage, just a little spill. Not even one broken stem. Don't worry, these will be just fine.'

Even through the tears she recognised the untidy nails of a fellow gardener. It wouldn't have mattered if his hands had been meticulously scrubbed and manicured, she would have known by the careful way he rescued the little basil plants, taking them gently by their stems and placing them back in the compost.

'There, you see? Good as new.' He placed the tray on the table next to the basket of veg. 'Lovely veg, by the way,' he added. 'The courgettes are exquisite. Did you grow them?' He picked up the one that had been shoved up her cunt only minutes before and she burst into tears again. A courgette! She had actually been reduced to fucking a courgette.

'Oh dear. Oh God. I'm so sorry.'

She scrabbled off the stool to make a run for it,

anywhere but here, someplace where she could hide her humiliation. 'Wait! Don't run off like that.' He slipped an arm around her and caught her before she could flee. 'I'm sorry. I'm really, really sorry. Please at least give me a chance to apologise.'

'No, no. It's not you,' she sobbed against his shoulder. 'You have nothing to apologise for. You're doing great, wonderful, actually. It's me. I'm so stupid. So absolutely stupid.'

'Don't be ridiculous. I know stupid when I see it, and you're not it.' He tightened his arms around her and she felt good solid muscle in the embrace. God, how long had it been since she felt good solid male muscle? She slipped her arms around his neck. He was tall and, as he tightened his embrace, he practically lifted her off her feet. Tall and strong, she thought, as the muscles low in her belly gave a little quiver.

One large hand began to stroke her mussed hair. She hadn't worn it back today because Dan liked it loose, but Dan never touched it. This bloke was touching it, gently, tenderly, the same way he'd touched her seedlings. Her nipples beaded to a tight, nearly painful press against the rise and fall of his chest. She could feel the heat of his breath against the top of her ear, breath which seemed to have accelerated a bit. He continued, 'In fact, if that veg garden I walked past is your doing, then I'd say you're anything but stupid. You're an artist. I'm in awe.'

15

Then she did the unthinkable. She curled her fingers in his thick brown hair and pulled his face down to hers. A little sigh of surprise escaped his throat, but he didn't resist. Still standing on tiptoe, she brushed her lips across his. Not only did he not resist, but he returned the favour, cupping her cheek in his large hand and lifting her off her feet with the arm that now encircled her waist. The brush of lips became a full-fledged assault, tongues sparring, lips crushing, breath coming in harsh little gasps. And it wasn't just the mouth. It was the overall effect of a real body, a real live male body barely able to contain the erection she could now clearly feel through his jeans. And just from the rub up, it made the courgette seem rather inadequate.

'I don't know you nearly well enough for this,' he said when he finally came up for air. But before she could apologise for her unacceptable behaviour, his mouth was up for round two. This time, he lifted her bodily on to the staging table, her legs falling open on either side of him, her dress scrunching until rough denim raked the moist satin gusset of her knickers.

'You've rescued my seedlings and fondled my courgette. That's good enough for me,' she breathed against his mouth.

She was just getting ready to open his fly and free Simba when Cook called from the garden path.

'Francie? Francie, are you there?'

They barely managed to straighten themselves and look like they were engaged with the seedlings when a heavy-set woman in a pink track suit huffed through the greenhouse door all aflutter and already in full conversation mode. 'There you are, Francie. Ms Bel says I'm not cooking enough vegetables. That silly massage therapist of hers says she should eat more, can you believe it? If the woman eats any more vegetables, she'll be taking up residence in the toilet. Last I heard diarrhoea wasn't an anti-ageing treatment, but what do I know? I'm just the cook. Oh, hello.' She addressed the man next to Francie with a smile of approval, and smoothed her always frizzy hair with a flutter of her hand. 'And who might you be?'

'I might be Simon, Simon Paris. I'm here to see Dan … er … Mr Alexander, about the Renaissance garden he's planning.'

'He and Ms Bel just got home a few minutes ago.' Cook nodded towards the big house rising above the shrubbery and trees. 'You can walk back with me if you'd like.'

'If you give me a second, I'll pot up a couple of basil plants for you to take back with you,' Francie said, when she'd caught her breath.

'Oh, lovely, lovely,' the woman said. 'I'll just have a wander around, see what's ready, and get some ideas for next week's menus.' She turned on her heels and disappeared into the veg patch.

Before Francie knew what was happening, Simon found the dibber and the nesting terracotta pots she had planned to use for the basil then brought them to where the rescued plants perched on the table looking no worse for their tumble. 'You OK?' He asked, as she busied herself transplanting the seedlings, trying to salvage what little dignity remained to her.

'Fine,' she said. 'Fine. Sorry about that. Just not a good day and, well, I'm a bit sensitive about my seedlings.'

'I can understand that,' he said, filling the pots with the mix of compost and grit she'd made up for the seedlings earlier. His hands were large and rough and clearly used to hard work. It was only then, only after she'd managed to regain some composure that she had time to properly take in the rest of the package. His faded but clean T-shirt bore the words 'Renaissance Gardens' in flowing italic script stretched just tightly enough over one mounded pec to convince Francie that what was underneath would be as much a pleasure to look at as it was to be pressed up against. She glanced up into startling grey eyes which offset a spattering of sun-browned freckles, all balanced by a broad smile that might well have been the warmest thing she'd felt all day. All in all he was a lovely specimen of maleness that, when combined with the adept way he dealt with her seedlings and her physical attack on his person, made her feel a whole lot better.

18

'I'm very sensitive about anything I've nurtured and tended to,' he was saying by the time she got her eyes up past the nice chest to the equally nice face. 'And these are lovely seedlings, sturdy, healthy, not leggy.'

'Then you're a gardener,' she said.

'I own a landscaping business.' He nodded to the logo on his shirt. 'Sadly I don't have as much time to devote to my little veg plot as I'd like, but I manage a tomato or two and a few runner beans, you know. That sort of thing.'

'Don't suppose you'd be hiring, would you?'

He looked up at her. 'Are you serious? You'd leave this?' He gestured around him.

She swallowed hard, afraid she would cry again. 'I have my reasons. I can do more than kitchen gardening. I've done a bit of landscaping myself, though I have to say the veggies are my first love.'

'But you want to leave all this and work somewhere else?'

Just then Cook stepped back in. 'Tomatoes and coriander look just perfect for a nice dhal, and we've not had a good curry in a while. Oh, and the aubergines are lovely. I'll send you a list.' She nestled two of the newly transplanted basil plants into the end of the basket and motioned to Simon. 'I'll take you up to the house now.'

He turned to Francie, brushed a fingertip over the back of her hand, just out of Cook's view, and held her in his steamy grey gaze. 'Lovely to meet you, Francie. I hope we can talk gardening again sometime soon.' Then he turned and followed Cook out of the greenhouse, leaving Francie to admire the exquisite way his arse filled out the seat of his jeans and contemplate what had just happened.

Chapter Three

There was plenty of wine to wash down what Dan was sure must be far too many vegetables, though he did find the courgettes particularly tasty. Extra wine would help ease him into the night's entertainment, as Bel had called it. She was already next to him on the sofa in the lounge, leaning over his lap stroking his cock through his trousers. It was responding nicely, with the help of a few thoughts of Francie's lovely round bottom.

'You like that, don't you?' Bel whispered against his ear, her voice gone all throaty and porn-starry. 'You like it when I play with your cock, don't you, darling?'

He wondered if she expected the porn-star response: 'Fuck yeah, baby, play with my cock!' Instead he just moaned something like 'mmmmrrrhp' as she undid his trousers and extricated his penis with scary long nails that always made him a bit nervous. Then she went to work on him with her mouth.

Even in his surly mood, there was no denying Bel was good with her mouth. It wasn't long before she had him rocking and grinding against the sofa, his fingers curled in her honey-brown hair. Wasn't it platinum blonde just last week? Who could remember from one day to the next?

She had just pulled back to lift her top over her head, when he stopped her. 'Not here, Bel. The servants might see.'

'Who cares?' she said.

But as she made a second effort, he grabbed her wrist and stood, pulling her to her feet. 'I care. Come on. Up to the bedroom with you.' She cursed under her breath as he herded her towards the stairs, struggling to stash his erection.

Upstairs in the bedroom, he tried to pull her to him, but she shrugged him off. 'I have to go change.' As she trotted off to the bathroom, even he had to admit she was lovely when she was pouting. While she rattled about at her ablutions, he stripped off his clothes. He started to get into his pajamas, thought better of it, and crawled into bed in only his boxers. He stroked his cock absently as he listened to water running, and wondered why Bel could never be spontaneous like Francie was. Thinking about her, skirt up, legs open, cunt swollen and exposed, made his balls feel full and heavy, even though he'd only been with her and had a good emptying just a few hours ago. But oh God, even the thought of her with that big-arsed courgette up her hole made him hot.

Bel interrupted his thoughts as she came out of the bathroom in a very tiny, very sheer lace bra with matching stockings and suspenders. And a fucking towel! Which she spread on her side of the bed. 'Sally just changed the sheets,' she said. 'We don't want to get them messy, do we?'

'Of course not. We wouldn't want that, would we?' He forced a smile and patted the bed, on top of the spread towel.

She lay back next to him, careful to smooth her hair across the pillow. Then she gave him a heavy-lidded look and began stroking a nipple to a stiff peak beneath the thin lace.

He thought of Francie's lovely breasts, and his mouth watered. He pushed aside the strap of her bra, lifted a tit free and began to suck and tongue the nipple and areola.

'Mmmm,' she moaned. 'You like my tits?'

She knew he did. When they were first married it was all about her tits, her luscious, heavy, large-nippled tits. Back then, he couldn't keep his hands off them. He still couldn't, he supposed, at least not when she presented them to him so brazenly. He shoved the bra down until he could cup both her breasts, then he buried his face between them. He could suffocate in their deep soft cleavage, and in the past he had done his best to do just that. He had licked them, sucked them, spanked them, pinched them and fucked the valley between them until he had exploded in heavy spurts into Bel's mouth. And she had sucked him dry like she was a baby at nursing time.

Now, all he could think of was doing the same thing to Francie, though her breasts were smaller, the squeeze would be tighter, but he'd be slick from the licking she would give him beforehand. His balls clenched at the thought.

Bel guided his hand down between her legs, sliding his fingers into the familiar pouting folds of her pussy. 'I'm so wet for you,' she breathed against the top of his head. She was creamy and heavy, and her clit strained against his thumb as he probed her. Her eyelids fluttered and her breath hitched, and he couldn't wait any longer, thinking of Francie as he was. He freed his cock over the top of his boxers, crawled in between her legs and pushed home. She uttered a little cry as he began to thrust, concentrating hard on the vision of Francie's lovely cunt full to the hilt with the courgette, imagining it was his cock pushing into her instead.

* * *

Damn it! Bel was so tired of Dan climbing on to her silently and going at it. Oh, he always made her come, or rather she made herself come, but it was getting harder and harder not to just fake it and be done with it. She should have known better than to ask for sex tonight. She could have slept in *her* bedroom, like she usually did these days, and had a good go with her vibe. It would have been easier.

She wrapped her legs around his waist to at least get a little stimulation against her clit where she needed it.

'Shall I play with your clit?' he asked between gritted teeth.

'No,' she grunted. 'No, I'm all right.' He was getting close, she could tell. He might have to finish her off with his fingers if he came first, and she hated that. She hated trying to come with him nodding off, with his mind who knew where, but wherever it was, it definitely wasn't on what he was doing to her. She shifted again to get more friction and gripped his cock tighter, straining from the effort of pressing up to meet him,

The thought came uninvited into her head, but suddenly it was there: Ellen with the little droplets of sweat glistening against the lovely pert tops of her breasts, Ellen with her nipples pressing against the pink French-cut T-shirt that did little to disguise her lack of a bra. Ellen missing Bel's cheek with her goodbye kiss, after her massage, and settling it firmly, not fleetingly but firmly, on Bel's lips. Then there was that lovely opportunistic tongue darting in to take advantage of Bel's surprised gasp. And suddenly they were tongue-dancing, mouth to mouth, breast to breast, body to body, and Bel damn near came in her panties from the sheer pleasure of it.

Her pussy gushed at the thought and clamped down tight on Dan's cock. He gave a hard grunt in response, and she thrust up to meet him with renewed energy.

She'd hurried away from her massage session all flustered and confused. Oh, Ellen had offered an embarrassed apology, but in the car on the drive home Bel had come, with her fingers raking at the crotch of her knickers, while sitting there in traffic, thinking about Ellen's luscious mouth, thinking about the feel of Ellen's titties against hers. And oh, how she had come! It had been so easy. And now, with Dan tensing at the approach of his orgasm, she thought about what would have happened if she had slid Ellen's hand up under her skirt. Would the woman have fingered her wet pussy? Would she have guided Bel's hand to return the favour? And what would it feel like to diddle another woman's cunt? God, she suddenly wanted to know.

'I'm coming,' Dan gasped, with a thrust that felt like it would go clear through her.

Thinking hard of how it felt to come on her own fingers, knowing just how soft and warm and wet a woman's vulva is when she's aroused, thinking about

Ellen's sweet lips, she gripped his cock with her cunt, bore down hard and tumbled over the edge with him.

* * *

Francie would have laughed at the irony of the situation if the joke hadn't been on her. Her bedroom window faced Dan's bedroom window. She knew that because he told her. He told Francie that there were nights when Bel was asleep that he would stand in front of the window and masturbate thinking of her. There had even been nights when they'd seen each other, and she had stood naked, wanting to show herself to him. Oh, she knew he could barely see her at that distance. But while he masturbated, he would know that she was naked with her fingers dancing over her clit and dipping between her labia while she thought of him. And she wanted him to know that.

But he wasn't at the window tonight. He was fucking his wife. She felt that knowledge with an ache that was almost physical. She felt it down low between her hipbones. And she was horny. It really pissed her off that, for some stupid-arsed reason, knowing the two of them were humping and grinding and grunting made her outrageously horny, even as it ripped her heart out.

She untied the knot that held her robe closed around her waist and let it slide off her shoulders. Her breasts felt heavy and full, and the cool breeze blowing in the window made her nipples pucker and stretch. She could smell her pussy, like a warm brimming tide pool. She slipped two fingers in between her folds and felt her silky slip and slide yield to the touch. She wondered if Simon had smelled her when he found her in the greenhouse, all wet and slippery from just coming. Surely he had. How could he not?

Oh God, Simon. He had made the rest of her day bearable. If Cook hadn't interrupted, would he have fucked her right there on the staging table in the greenhouse? She wouldn't have needed a courgette. She smiled as she thought of the size of his cock pressing so anxiously against the thin fabric of her panties. Would he have actually fucked her, though? Or would he have been a gentleman and perhaps asked her out for drinks first?

And what about her? Would she have let him take her, knowing why he was in the position in the first place, knowing that her tears and her distress had motivated him, that she had thrown herself at him like some brazen slut. And yet he certainly wasn't put off by her advances. He seemed happy to take it to the next level. And he was a gardener. Good with his hands. She could tell that by the way he handled her seedlings. She wondered what else he could do with those lovely hard hands. Her pussy gripped and pouted, gripped and pouted against the scissoring of her fingers, and her clit felt like it would burst with its fullness.

She looked out at the darkened window of Dan's room. Then, thinking of Simon rubbing against her crotch with his heavy erection, she leaned her back against the window frame and perched on the sill, carefully moving aside the hefty forest cactus cascading in the moonlight. Once she was settled, she lifted one leg on to the sill and opened herself lewdly, imagining what might have happened if she'd had time to undo Simon's trousers, release his hard-on and shove aside the insubstantial crotch of her already wet panties. He was right there, so close, so ready. And she was slick and swollen. He would have barely had to do anything but shift his hips slightly. She would have guided him in, in deep and hard and tight. Then she would have laid back on the table, wrapped her legs around him and watched him through the shafts of sunlight flooding the greenhouse. She would have watched him thrust and shove and grunt until he came, until they both came, and that empty spot for Dan would somehow not be quite so empty any more. In her mind's eye, she imagined what Simon's lovely face would look like when his body tightened in the throes of an ejaculation. And with a gush of wetness and a shudder that nearly knocked the plant off the sill and shook her to the core, she came on her fingers, imagining that she'd been riding Simon Paris's cock, while Dan looked on longingly from just outside the greenhouse door.

Chapter Four

Ellen Martin went to the homes of her more exclusive clients. They paid her a lot for the privilege. She was that good. But Bel enjoyed going for her massage at the health club surrounded by the sweaty metal-and-leather atmosphere of the gym. OK, it was an exclusive club, and it never really smelled like sweat, but the atmosphere was still there. Today the workout had been particularly hard. The shower afterwards was cool and bracing, but it hadn't been enough to take Bel's mind off Ellen's kiss or the fact that it had been thoughts of Ellen that had sent her over the edge last night when she had sex with Dan.

She hadn't been able to sleep afterwards, and when she finally did, long towards morning, she dreamed of Ellen. The dreams were super-heated, with visions of Bel nursing at Ellen's lovely breasts while Ellen stroked and caressed between her swollen labia; of Ellen's lovely mouth lapping and nipping and sucking its way down over Bel's breasts and belly and right on into her pussy. In the morning, the need was so great that Bel had had to bring herself off while she was sitting on the toilet.

There had been no planned massage for the day, and she seldom came to the gym two days in a row, but she couldn't resist. A little extra exercise was always a good thing, Bel convinced herself, and luckily Ellen had a light day and could fit her in.

Surely Ellen could figure out that it wasn't a massage she really wanted. The problem was, Bel wasn't actually sure what she did want. She didn't want to cheat on her husband, and God knows there had been plenty of opportunities. She wasn't unaware of the looks and the come-ons of other men. She knew she was an attractive woman, but she was also a faithful woman. Bored, but faithful. She figured if Dan could endure the boredom, so could she. And in truth she had never been tempted before Ellen's kiss.

But somewhere last night in the tossing and turning and listening to Dan snore, before she tiptoed off to her own bedroom, the thought had come to her as clear as daylight: how could it actually be cheating if she were with another woman? There'd be no penetration, no testosterone, nothing for Dan to be jealous of really. In fact Dan, being a typical bloke, would probably really get off on the idea of two women going at it. And it wasn't like she would actually fall in love with Ellen or anything like that. It was just sex. It wasn't even real sex, right? It was two girls fooling around. It meant nothing really. Other than the fact that she might actually get some satisfaction that didn't involve the same old, same old she endured with Dan a few times a month.

She would never look at another man. She took her marriage vows very seriously. It was just, well, their sex life was such a bore, and she was a sexual woman. She had needs, needs she had been perfectly happy to take care of with her growing collection of sex toys, but then Ellen had kissed her. OK, she had to admit she'd harboured secret thoughts about Ellen even before the kiss. She had thoughts of Ellen's tight nipples popping out of the top of her vest, thoughts of Ellen's lovely massaging hands moving right on down over her belly and in between her legs. She'd made herself come to those very thoughts more than once. But they were just fantasies. Everyone had fantasies. On the other hand, who would know better how a woman likes her breasts touched and her nipples fondled than another woman? Who would know better how a woman likes her clitoris stroked and the creamy valley deep between her labia fingered and probed than another woman? And who could possibly know what to do with her hands better than a massage therapist? Once the thought had planted itself in Bel's brain, and between her legs, she couldn't get rid of it.

So here she was shaking like a leaf, drying herself from the shower, but knowing even the thick Egyptian cotton of the towel wasn't going to take care of the wet condition of her pussy. Ellen was waiting in the next room. Ellen would know what she wanted. Ellen would see it in her eyes. Ellen would smell her heat, and no amount of lingering in the shower could wash the smell of her lust away, not when she could barely stand up from the weight of her arousal.

With hands that were trembling, she tied the sash of the thin linen robe around her waist, checked her hair and took a deep breath.

She barely managed a soft rap on the door before Ellen opened it. 'Isabel, sweetheart, are you all right?' This time there was the proper distance and the kiss on each cheek. The massage table was spread with fresh linen, and everything seemed strangely normal, which made a cold knot tighten below Bel's breastbone. Had their kiss meant nothing to Ellen? Had she been just a stupid, needy woman fantasising about what Ellen had already forgotten, making something out of nothing?

'Goodness, you're tense,' Ellen said caressing Bell's shoulder and offering her a concerned smile. 'I wouldn't have thought it possible after I gave you such a thorough going over yesterday.'

Such a thorough going over, indeed, Bel thought.

'Bel, darling, is everything all right?' she asked again.

Bel nodded dumbly and, for an uncomfortable second her chin quivered, and she thought she might cry.

Ellen lifted Bel's chin and held her in a knowing gaze. 'Don't worry, sweetie. I'll take care of it. I'll make you feel better.' She nodded to the table, and offered a smile that was a whole lot more than just sympathetic.

Shaking like she'd come apart, Bel brazenly opened her sash and let the robe puddle on the floor around her feet, her gaze locked on Ellen's lovely hazel eyes.

'If you're this tight all over, darling, perhaps we need to try a different approach today. Lie down on your back for me, if you would.'

Feeling every bit as naked as she was, Bel did as she was told.

Ellen slipped out of the white uniform jacket she wore, revealing the spaghetti-strapped pink vest that beautifully displayed her workout-sculpted arms and her usual lack of a bra. Then she did something that, in all the time Bel had been coming to her, she had never done before. She locked the door. Her fingers lingered on the lock for a second, then she turned and walked to the table. 'Bel, you're not actually here for a massage, are you?'

Before Bel could make up some lame excuse, Ellen lifted her vest over her head in one smooth, nearly elegant move that took Bel's breath away. Actually, it was the sight of Ellen's exquisite breasts, nipples pressing hard at the forefront, that took Bel's breath away, made her for a split second unable to focus on what Ellen was saying. Something about it being OK.

'I've wanted you for a long time, Bel,' she was saying. 'And I thought you wanted me too, but I wasn't sure until I threw caution to the wind yesterday.' She cupped her breasts and stroked her nipples. Bel's nipples tensed in empathy, a response Ellen didn't miss.

'There are other ways I can make you feel good, Bel.' She slid her yoga trousers and thong down over her thighs and stepped out of them. 'There are ways that are even better than massage.' She stood so close to the table that Bel could have reached out and touched her tightly trimmed pubic curls. It was all she could do to lie still on the table under the woman's hungry gaze.

'You need some relief, don't you, darling? I can tell by the way you hold the tension in your body, all of it right down here.' She laid a warm hand on Bell's abdomen just millimetres above her pubis then pressed softly. Bel couldn't help it; she shifted her hips to raise her mound closer, and Ellen smiled knowingly. 'Oh, sweetheart, you're so needy. We women tend to hold so much energy down here, down where our creative centre is.' She slid a hand down to cup the smooth flesh of Bel's mound and Bel nearly came off the table.

'Ssh! Ssh. There, there, darling. I know what you need.

Just let me make you feel better.' For what seemed like a maddening eternity, Ellen pressed and stroked and massaged all the area below Bel's navel. And Bel, well, she didn't handle the situation with as much dignity and aplomb as she would have liked. She couldn't seem to control the little whimpers and gasps that gathered deep in her chest right below her breasts then rose in little waves of longing up through her throat, while her hips tightened and shifted against the heel of Ellen's palm, still just above her pubic bone.

'There, there, darling,' Ellen crooned. 'Just relax and let it happen. It's all right if you touch your breasts if you need to. It's all right. That's it, sweetheart, cup them, stroke your lovely nipples. Ah, such exquisite breasts, and so responsive, aren't they? I bet your husband likes to fuck them, doesn't he?'

Bel groaned and nodded dumbly.

'If I had a cock, that's what I'd want to do, while your little pink tongue darted in and out over the head of my penis every time I thrust.'

Even in her fevered state, Bel noticed Ellen's left hand had migrated down between her own legs. Bel couldn't see what she was doing, but the tight rhythmic knotting and shifting of the muscles in her forearm and the quiver and dance of her breasts told her everything she needed to know.

'Of course if I had a cock, there are other places I'd

want to put it first before I fucked your lovely breasts.' With that the hand that had been massaging her abdomen moved down over Bel's mound and the slender middle finger gave her clit a tweak that nearly sent Bel into orbit.

'Open your legs for me, sweetheart,' Ellen whispered. 'That's it, darling. Let me massage you where you really need it, where you've needed it for ages.'

Bel opened her legs and shifted ever so slightly towards Ellen to give her better access. With her thumb working Bel's clit to a raw nub of heat, the woman slipped her middle and index finger down between Bell's labia and gasped. 'My goodness, Isabel, is all of this creamy slippery lushness for me?'

Bell whimpered and nodded and shifted closer to the delicious fingers.

Ellen offered a throaty chuckle, then gave an inward and upward thrust and a hard rub right against Bel's G-spot, and Bel drenched the table in a flood of heat that would have embarrassed her if she'd been in bed with Dan. But Ellen shoved her legs wide apart and pushed her face in so close that Bel could feel her breath coming fast and hard against her pout. 'Oh my God, Bel, you're exquisite,' she whispered. 'I've never seen another woman really wet herself with her girly juices. Please, let me look. I need to see you.' And as she spoke, she applied more pressure to Bel's G-spot and Bel gushed again and nearly came off the table with an orgasm that

37

had her writhing and twisting, thighs clasping involuntarily around Ellen's face.

Ellen made no effort to push Bel's legs open; instead she settled there in the vice-grip of Bel's thighs, sniffing and inhaling. Her hands had moved to knead and release, knead and release Bel's arse cheeks. 'Mmmm, you smell heavenly, darling. I smell you every time I massage you. Afterwards I always have to leave time between you and the next client so I can take care of my own pussy, and I always come thinking about tasting your juicy fanny that smells so delicious.' She nipped the inside of Bel's thigh. Bel opened her legs with a little gasp, and Ellen cupped her buttocks and pulled her right up close to her mouth. And the mouth that had kissed Bel's lips so deliciously yesterday now kissed and licked her girly lips equally deliciously.

Bel curled her fingers in Ellen's soft copper hair and bore down until she was amazed that the woman could even breathe. And that wonderful tongue felt like it had somehow licked and stroked and danced right up inside her, while her mouth tugged and suckled at Bel's labia and her clit with little nips that made her wet herself anew from the sheer pleasure of it. Surely there would have been a lake beneath her undulating bottom had not Ellen's greedy mouth lapped and sucked and slurped her wetness like she was some piece of juicy, ripe fruit, split in two, dripping and swollen and begging to be eaten.

It was a good thing the table was sturdy because the orgasms had graduated from tremors to convulsions and, in what might have been an effort to keep her client safely on the table, Ellen crawled her way up Bel's body, kissing and nipping as she went, until she was well and truly on top of her, breast to breast, pubis to pubis and mouth to mouth.

'Taste how yummy you are,' Ellen breathed, coming up from a deep tongue kiss. 'I've never tasted anything so sumptuous.'

Bel had tasted herself before, but only tentatively on the tips of her fingers after masturbating, nothing like the wet, fecund taste of her on another woman's face, on another woman's mouth.

'And now, let's come together,' Ellen sighed. She shifted until her thigh was in between Bel's legs, pressing up tight against her client's sopping pussy, then she wriggled and manoeuvred until Bel's thigh was equally pressed between her legs, up tight against the heat of her, the split of her, the unbelievably soft wet of her. Then she began to undulate and writhe. Bel mirrored her motions, shifting her hips, pressing her thigh, tightening her legs against the leg that rubbed her cunt, as Ellen did the same. Undulation became hard shifting. Hard shifting gave way to flat-out thrusting and pumping accompanied by animal grunts and growls, and the table shook beneath them. Muscles tensed and stretched tight. All breathing stopped, and the room was sucked dry of everything but raw, super-heated need. And when Bel was sure she would die in the agony of pleasure, in the bruising vice-grip of Ellen's thighs, everything shattered and broke apart in a kaleidoscope of colours. Heatwaves and shudders rose up from the centre of both women in the explosion of their release. Each smothered the other in wet kisses and humid giggles before falling limp and breathless in a tangle of arms and legs.

Chapter Five

Simon's last appointment had cancelled, so he was at Dan's almost two hours earlier than they were scheduled to meet. But it was all right. Dan had given him the gate code and told him to feel free to wander about and get to know the place. He wanted a proper Renaissance garden, and it was going to be a big one. Typical of Dan Alexander. He never did things by halves. He hadn't when he and Simon had been at uni together, and apparently he still didn't. Simon didn't mind, though. Getting to know this space would be a pleasure. It was a good thing, because he'd be spending a lot of time in it for a while.

It was a lovely space, very hilly and scrubby in places, with lots of havens for birds and wildlife, which he intended not only to leave but to enhance. It was a challenge he was looking forward to. In his mind, he could already see where the topiary maze would be and where he would place the big fountain, the centrepiece of the garden. It was like seeing a landscape appearing through the rising mist. It was always like that when he had the opportunity to create an outdoor space that was both beautiful and useful.

Back when they were at uni, he and Dan had spent time in Italy together at the Villa d'Este in Tivoli. Dan had been there just for fun, while Simon had gone to study the garden itself, in as much detail as he could manage in one month. Both men had fallen in love with the place. Well, Dan had fallen in love with a young Italian docent, actually. While Simon studied the hydraulics of the fountains and the layout of the topiary on the hillsides, Dan and Gabriella found all the secret places to fuck.

Perhaps Dan wanted to recapture those carefree days once again, only this time with his wife. After all, the garden was being designed as a scaled-down version of the Villa d'Este. Simon smiled to himself. He'd make sure there were lots of nice little hidey-holes where Dan and his wife could fuck. The smile broadened, and the rise of his cock tightened his jeans as he thought about his encounter with Dan's lovely kitchen gardener. He wouldn't mind trying out a few of those hidey-holes with her, just to make sure they would serve the purpose. He definitely planned to ask Dan about her. He'd already had a few fantasies that involved what would happen after he'd asked her out for drinks and dinner, or after they'd shared gardening tips down on their knees between her lovely rows of French beans.

Simon brought a small sketch pad along and, as he walked, he sketched. He already knew where he wanted to put the grotto and the sculpture of *Diana at the Hunt* that Dan had commissioned. Wow, he must really adore Isabel to build her such an extravagant garden. Simon had never met Dan's wife. In fact he was surprised when Dan had called him up after all this time. When they left uni, they had drifted apart. The spoilt little rich boy went back to the manor and Simon started land-scaping. He had found his niche in decorative gardens and in restoring gardens in ageing manors. He was very good at what he did so it probably wasn't all that surprising that Dan would call him for the job.

* * *

'Francie? Francie, are you there?'

This time she wasn't hard to find, nor did she seem angry. She offered him a relaxed smile. She could have been his *Diana at the Hunt* standing there under the big oak tree, clothed only in a thin wraparound dress, hair falling free from the large clip that that couldn't quite contain her unruly tresses. She was examining some delicate daisy-like flower between her chlorophyll-stained fingers. Dan's cock jerked in his trousers. She had come from the veg patch. She would smell of loam and lovely female sweat and green growing things. And underneath it all, she would smell of sumptuous female heat. He always made sure, even though he never touched her, that he was close enough to smell her, close enough to take in the intoxicating cocktail of her complex scent.

She looked up at him from under thick lashes, crushed the flower in her hand and held it up to his nose, careful not to touch him. 'Wild camomile,' she said. 'It makes lovely tea.'

He inhaled the clean astringent scent just as she dropped the crushed flower, removed the clip from her hair and combed the scent, still heavy on her hand, through her thick locks. It was all he could do to keep from pulling her into his arms.

He leaned, practically fell, against the trunk of the tree, turned until his back was pressed tight against it and fought with his fly, uttering a sound that was almost wild as he touched himself and lifted his penis free.

The slight breeze lifted her hair, then toyed with the folds of her skirt, teasing him with just the smallest glimpse of what lay beneath. It was then that he realised the dress was only held in place by a thin ribbon tied just below her right breast.

'You've been thinking about me.' She nodded lightly at his erection, which he now stroked to full length.

'Oh yes. I've been thinking about you. I'm always thinking about you.'

As she watched his stroking grow more enthusiastic, she absently slipped one hand inside the criss-cross bodice of the dress to stroke and caress a breast. But that wasn't enough. She shoved the dress open until her breasts were free, and began to knead hard and tug at her nipples. She moved close to him, so close that she was nearly touching him. Then she inhaled. 'You smell horny, Dan. You smell like dark thick man lust.'

Oh dear God, then the woman squatted, legs wide apart, so wide the dress gave up any efforts at coverage, and her lovely swollen pussy was fully and lewdly on display. But he only caught a quick view of it. Then she leaned in close, right in front of him, so close that the breeze brushed her hair against his cock, so close that he could feel the heat of her breath, so close that he really thought she would take his cock in her mouth. And at that moment, if she had done so, there would have been no way in hell he would have had the will to pull away from her, faithful or not. He stood there tight, holding his breath, balls aching with their weight, cock stretched in anticipation. Not for the first time, he wished she'd just take the choice out of his hands so he could say it just happened. It wasn't his fault.

But instead of taking his cock in her mouth, she inhaled deeply, her nose pressed in close to, but not quite touching, the space between his erect penis and his balls, the place usually tucked tidily away under his resting cock. And for a second it was all he could do to keep from unloading in her hair and down her spine.

'Mmmm, you can fool everyone but me, Daniel Alexander. You may dress and act the part. You may even have been born to it, but I smell you. Underneath it all you smell like an animal, an animal who wants to fuck, just like the rest of us animals.'

Then she dropped even lower on her haunches, sniffing and groaning, and there was nothing for it but to shove frantically at his trousers and boxers, to give her more of him to sniff. God, he wanted her to take his scent. Sweet Christ, he wanted her to take so much more.

She inhaled great gulping gasps of his smell. The hand not kneading her breast caressed her tight pubic curl, then slid down to press up into her slick snatch. And it was his turn to sniff the air, wishing like hell he could bury his face in her delicious cunny and cover himself in her hot sticky scent.

As though she'd read his thoughts, as though she knew his hunger, she lifted her fingers, glistening with her juices, up for him to inhale, and his cock jerked and surged, but he held himself back. Then she pulled her fingers to her lips and sucked them. 'Mmm,' she sighed. 'Do you ever taste yourself, Dan? Do you ever taste the flavour of your come when it's been warmed in Bel's pussy and blended with her cunt juices? Do you ever lap up all that lovely blended ambrosia? If you haven't you should. Pussy juice and semen taste best together. And me –' she ran her hands down over her breasts and her belly then spread her labia wide '– me, I like that luscious blended heat all over my body, everywhere. I'd bathe in it if I could.' She alternated rubbing the flat of each hand in turn up against the splay of her cunt. Then she wiped the resulting moisture down the insides of her thighs.

Dear God, the woman was driving him insane! He watched, feeling like his balls would burst, and yet pressing his thumb like a vice to the underside of his penis, wanting to hold his load, wanting to wait and watch and inhale and listen.

'We miss so much, Dan. We humans miss so much.' This time she bore down hard on her hand, and he could see the juices dribbling between her fingers, dripping on to the grass. He could smell her urgency. Then she brought the hand dripping with her heat up to cup her bare breast, then stroke and rub right on up her chest like she was massaging herself with expensive lotion. And the next wet hand shoved through her hair, over her face and down her neck. It was as though the woman before him transformed into something feral. She lay down on the grass and rolled from side to side, her skirt bunching up

47

over her hips, her legs wide apart, her clit protruding from the apex of her gape like a deep-red cherry. Then she was writhing and squirming and bucking against the flat of her hand, against three, then four fingers shoved so hard into her cunt hole that he would have thought it would hurt. She rubbed and bucked and whimpered, pinching first her nipples, then her clit, then spreading more of her juices over her body, over her raised buttocks, over her hips. It took him a second to realise that she was orgasming, orgasming in a wet, juicy, writhing flood there on the grass. And it was enough. He could hold back his own flood no more.

Suddenly she was standing beside him, the smell of her nearly overwhelming in its delicious heat. She whispered in his ear, so close her lips nearly touched him. 'That's it, Dan, let the animal loose, even if it's just in your head. You can do that with me. And you know it, and that's why you want me.'

Then, out of nowhere, Simon Paris came sauntering up to them. 'Hi Dan, Francie, I wasn't expecting to see you two here yet. I know I'm early, but I –' He stopped in his tracks, taking in first one of them then the other before he twigged. 'Oh shit.'

For the briefest of seconds, it was as though there were a sudden deep freeze, and everyone had been frozen solid. No one moved. No one breathed. Then everything exploded back into hot, uncomfortable real time.

'Oh God, I'm sorry.' Before Simon could turn to leave, Francie gave a little yelp of surprise, turned on her heels and fled like a deer through the thicket.

'No, wait, Simon,' Dan said, tucking himself in, his gaze following Francie until she disappeared. Then he cursed under his breath.

'Jesus, Dan, I'm so sorry.' He had caught Dan and Gabriella in a similar compromising situation back at the Villa d'Este all those years ago, but they'd just laughed and asked him to join them. He hadn't, of course. He'd been too shy. Though he'd often wished he had.

But Simon honestly was sorry this time. He really had liked Francie and was hoping to get to know her better. Just as well not, though. He shivered at the thought of how near he'd come, the other day in the greenhouse, to being pulled into the middle of what was not a very comfortable situation. The less he knew about the extra-marital affairs of his rich friends, the better, he figured.

'Not your fault,' Dan said, doing up his belt and running a hand through his hair, his gaze still on the place where Francie had disappeared. 'I shouldn't have had her meet me here, but I wanted her to see.'

'Then you're doing this for her.' Simon made a broad gesture around the hillside. She would appreciate it, at least as a gardener, he thought. But it somehow tainted the gift, that it was a gift to a mistress, that Dan's wife was just another cliché of the rich and bored.

Dan ran his fingers through his hair again and straightened his shirt. 'Yes. No. I don't know. I guess maybe.'

Simon shrugged. 'Listen, mate, it's none of my business. I just do the work. And I'm sorry I caught you and your mistress at a bad time.'

'She's not my mistress.'

In spite of himself Simon found a knot of anger tightening in his stomach that Dan didn't even have the guts to own up to the landscaper, a mere employee, that he was bonking the gardener. 'Right, and I'm Lady Gaga's hairdresser.'

Dan released a deflated sigh and scrubbed his hands over his face. 'I've really fucked things up, Simon.' He nodded towards the grassy slope of a hill that led to a stream at the bottom. 'Come on, walk with me.' Simon fell into step next to him.

They walked in silence until they were almost down to the stream, then Dan spoke. 'I'm crazy about her, Simon. She's my kitchen gardener, you know?'

Simon nodded. 'I met her the other day when I came to discuss the garden with you. She seemed really upset.' He thought it best to keep his method of comforting her to himself.

Dan groaned. 'It's all such a mess. I wasn't lying when I said she's not my mistress. Well, she's not my mistress in a physical sense. I'm faithful to my wife. We, Francie and I, only ever masturbate together.'

50

Simon couldn't hold back a snort of laughter, but the look Dan shot back stopped him mid-guffaw.

'I know what you think, and I know how utterly ridiculous that sounds, but I swear to you it's true. I'm crazy about the woman, but I pledged my troth to Bel.'

'You what?'

Dan shook his head and waved his hand as though he were batting away an insect. 'I made a promise, and I'll not break it. I'll stay faithful to Bel until I get the balls to ask her for a divorce. I'll not be like my father was.'

Simon studied Dan for a minute as they walked. 'And Francie's OK with this? Well, clearly she's not. I'm assuming it was you, your situation, she was upset about when I walked in on her at the greenhouse.'

'Of course she's not OK with it. That's the problem.'

'Then just ask Bel for a divorce,' Simon said.

'Oh, I will, I will. It's just now's a difficult time. I've got so much on my mind. And Bel's going through some difficult times too, and I just can't do it right now. It wouldn't be right.' He chuckled softly and shot Simon a sideways glance. 'Remember at Tivoli, when you caught me with Gabriella, and we asked you to join us.'

Simon smiled. 'It's like déjà vu, only you two weren't exactly having a wank, as I recall. One of the regrets of my youth, not joining your little party. Had a few good wanks thinking about it, though.'

It took Simon a second to realise Dan had stopped walking. He stood in knee-high grass, his brow drawn tight in deep concentration.

'What? What is it?' Simon backtracked to stand next to his friend.

'Maybe this time we need to turn the tables.' Dan stroked his chin thoughtfully. 'You know, alter the equation just slightly.'

'What? What tables, what equation?'

Dan began to walk again, slowly. 'What if Francie and I invited you to join us?'

'What?'

'Only this time I'd be the one having a wank. Oh, I'd be telling you what to do to her and all, or she'd be asking you, but think about it, Simon, how she must feel. She knows I still have sex with Bel. Granted, not very often, but I do my husbandly duty when she asks me.'

'Your husbandly duty. Right.'

'Well, I consider that a part of being faithful, wouldn't you?'

'Fuck, mate! You're asking the wrong person about that. How the hell would I know?'

'My point is that I get at least some sex because Bel is my wife, and I'm faithful to her. But poor Francie's faithful to me. She doesn't get anything but a wank, and she has to provide that for herself. I can't even touch her, Simon, because I'm afraid once I do I won't be able to stop myself. But if you, as my old and trusted friend, were to make love to her for me, you know, be my surrogate, then Francie could get some satisfaction too, and maybe ...'

'You want me to fuck your mistress for you?' Simon spoke through the hammering of his heart.

'Don't you think she's attractive?' Dan asked.

'Of course I think she's attractive. That's not the point. First of all, assuming that you really are certain you want me to have sex with your mistress while you watch and have a wank, what makes you think Francie would go for such a crazy scheme?'

'I could convince her,' Dan replied. 'We could convince her together. I know we could, Simon.'

Simon picked up the pace, feeling both horrified and aroused by the whole idea. 'I can't believe we're even having this conversation. What about Bel? What about your wife?'

Dan hurried to catch up. 'Well, Bel can hardly complain about Francie getting laid by a good-looking bloke like yourself. Bel's always trying to play matchmaker, and it pains her deeply that Francie doesn't have anyone. And if I catch the two of you together and end up having a wank, well, I can hardly be blamed for watching and enjoying, can I?'

For a brief moment, Simon recalled the feel of Francie

in his arms, the taste of her on his mouth, and his penis threatened unruliness. 'Look, Dan, I know we're old friends, but I'm here to build you a garden, not fuck your mistress for you, and I think it's best we keep it at that for the sake of all parties involved.'

Dan squared his shoulders and gave his throat a hard clearing. He was suddenly unable to meet Simon's gaze. 'Of course, mate. You're right. I forgot myself there for a minute. How about we just forget the whole conversation, pretend it never happened, all right?'

'Best thing to do, I think,' Simon said. But even as he said it, he couldn't quite get the vision out of his head of Francie with her legs wrapped around his waist.

Chapter Six

'We have to do something, Dan. We can't lose her now. She's finally got things the way we like them, and we really need her, and she's such a lovely person.' Bel burst into Dan's study in mid-sentence, like she always did. 'I wonder if it's something we've done. I thought she was happy here.' She wrung her hands and paced in front of his desk. 'Of course she's so quiet; it's hard to tell really. I just thought because the garden looked so fabulous and the vegetables have been so wonderful that she was content. Oh, Dan, that was selfish of me, wasn't it? Why didn't I consider what she might need? Because we can't lose her, you know. We just can't.'

'Bel ... Bel! Slow down. Sit down.' He came from behind his desk and settled his wife on the settee, then perched on the edge of it next to her. 'Now darling, calm down and tell me what you're on about.'

'It's Francie. Oh, Dan, Cook overheard her talking to someone about looking for another job. Darling, we can't let that happen. We just can't.'

Dan was glad he was sitting. He suddenly felt weak-kneed and dizzy. 'Are you sure? Is Cook sure?'

'Cook swears up and down that's what Francie said. Cook says she was talking to some guy about working for him. Oh, Dan, this is awful. This is just terrible. What are we going to do?'

Dan felt suddenly ill. It was his fault. He knew exactly why Francie would want to go somewhere else. It was totally his fault. But if Bel couldn't lose her, he certainly couldn't. He couldn't even think about it. He patted his wife on the thigh. 'Don't worry, sweetheart. I'll talk to her. I'll get to the bottom of the situation and make her an offer she can't refuse.' He forced what he hoped was a reassuring smile, but he didn't feel very reassured. He wanted to run out of the door this second and find her. He wanted to take her in his arms and beg her, take her in his arms and make it right. But he was no less married today than he was yesterday, and he couldn't possibly ask Bel for a divorce when she was so distraught. Anyway, he knew Francie wasn't home this morning. She had gone to the nursery for gooseberry plants or some such. Something Cook wanted, or something Bel's crazy masseuse had recommended. And Francie didn't trust the nursery or anyone else to pick them out for her. He loved that about her. He loved that she was uncompromising in her vocation.

'Don't worry, darling. I'll talk to her as soon as she gets back from the nursery. I promise.' He didn't tell Bel that he had already called Francie this morning early, like he always did on the days they met. She didn't answer. She never did. He just left a message on her mobile. He'd asked her to meet him in the rose garden. She never called him. She never made the arrangements. Instead she politely and quietly waited for him. She let him call the shots that affected her life as much as, if not more than, they did his. But, Jesus, he needed her! He'd find a way to make it up to her, he promised himself. Fortunately they'd have plenty of time before his meeting with Simon at the pub. By that time he'd have everything worked out with her, and then he'd be able to enjoy the first drawings Simon had done of the Renaissance garden. There'd be time. He'd figure out something. He had to.

* * *

Ellen was sitting across from Bel studying the menu. In fact anyone watching would have thought she had never read anything so fascinating. Bel, on the other hand, wasn't nearly as convincing, not when Ellen had kicked

off her red stiletto pumps and had managed, quite skil-
fully under their small table, to push Bel's knees apart,
shove up under her skirt and ease a groping foot in
between her thighs. Her big toe raked a satin trough
against Bel's French-cut knickers, up between Bel's pussy
lips, then pressed and circled her burgeoning clit. Each
time Ellen repeated the process, the trough in the satin
gusset deepened and became damper until Bel could feel
the fabric clinging from her perineum all the way to her
clit.

The waitress came to take their order, and Ellen
ordered a grilled salmon salad without missing a beat.

'Me too,' Bel said, trying to disguise a sudden spas-
modic jerk of her hips with a fake cough. 'I'll have that
toooo!'

After the waitress left, Ellen offered her a wicked smile.
'Interesting, the connection between cunt and nipples,
don't you think?' She gave a particularly deep prod with
her toe, and Bel moaned and wriggled her bottom closer
to the edge of the chair, glad of the long linen tablecloth
covering the scrunch of her skirt and the unladylike splay
of her legs. The restaurant was dimly lit, and they were
early, both facts that afforded them extra privacy. But
still Bel gave a quick glance around to make sure the
waitress was truly gone, before she worried open the top
few buttons of her thin silk blouse, holding Ellen's gaze
across the table. Just as Ellen gave a particular tantalising

stroke, she undid the front clasp of her bra, pushed aside one cup and shifted just enough for Ellen to get a clear view of her heavy nipple.

'Yes, amazing connection,' Ellen breathed, eyeing Bel's breast like it was her favourite dish. She caught her toe under the gusset of Bel's panties, then as easily as she would have with her fingers, she pulled the crotch aside. And suddenly her toe pushed home, parting Bel's swollen lips, in and out, in and out; then up and over the erection of Bel's clit, spreading her slippery goodness. In and out, in and out. All the while she stared at Bel's tit. Bel matched her rhythm with a subtle cup and knead, cup and knead, stroking her nipple with her thumb. She slowly worried her bottom lip with her teeth, and with a little-girl sigh she tightened her cunt muscles to grip and suck each time Ellen's toe slid home.

Ellen wriggled and shifted down in her seat. 'My pussy's soaking right through my panties,' she breathed.

'You must be going crazy,' Bel whispered. 'I wish my legs were longer.'

'I like your legs just like they are,' Ellen said with a nice deep thrust of her toe for emphasis. Then she pulled it out. 'Come on. Let's go to the ladies to freshen up a bit before our salads arrive.'

They barely made it inside the ladies' room before Ellen pushed Bel up against the wall and took her mouth in a hungry tongue-dance that made Bel's knees weak.

They were both vying for access to each other's knickers when they heard women's voices outside the door. Ellen grabbed Bel by the hand and hurried her into one of the stalls. Before she locked the door, she shoved open Bel's blouse, and her mouth clamped down hard enough on a nipple to make Bel whimper and stumble back, knocking the spare toilet roll off on to the floor with a soft ka-thunk. They stifled a wave of giggles as it rolled under the door leaving a white con trail behind it.

'I want to taste you,' Bel whispered. 'I want to taste your pussy.'

Ellen shoved her down to sit on the open toilet, then she manoeuvred her body in the tight space so she faced Bel. She shoved her short pencil skirt up over her hips, lifted one leg to rest on the top of the toilet-roll dispenser, and yanked the tiny crotch of her thong aside, wriggling it over one arse cheek as she thrust her hips forward. Suddenly Bel was face to face with Ellen's gaping slit. 'You've never eaten pussy before, have you, darling?' Ellen asked, curling her fingers in Bel's hair and guiding her closer to the delicious aroma that smelled so similar to her own cunt yet so intriguingly different.

Bel shook her head.

'It's all right, sweetie, don't be frightened. You'll like it, I promise.' With her other hand Ellen reached down and splayed her folds wide, pressing a finger along each side of her split so that the dark, begging hole at the centre pouted, open and inviting. The way her palm rested on her soft pubic curls and the way her fingers forced her lips open caused her heavy clit to protrude like an erect nipple. For a moment, Bel paused to explore with her eyes the womanscape displayed in shades of deep red and vein blue, darkening to blood-engorged purple in the delicate folds and crevices and the heavy swell of labial flesh. My God, Bel couldn't imagine a more exquisite sight.

Ellen lifted Bel's head with the firm curl of her fingers beneath her chin and kissed her, surprisingly gently. 'Honey, have you never looked at your own pussy?'

Bel shook her head dumbly.

Ellen tut-tutted softly. 'Oh, Bel, my lovely Bel, you have so much to learn.'

Bel tentatively leaned in and took Ellen's clit in her mouth. She felt the woman squirm, felt the nub of her tighten against her pursed lips, felt a warm flooding of moisture against her chin, felt her own pussy respond with its sympathetic flood. Carefully, she pulled away and pressed her index and middle finger to Ellen's hole, into the pearlescent slickness collecting there at the gaping edges. She pushed into the silky softness and marvelled at the quiver of Ellen's gape before it clamped down startlingly hard on her fingers, causing her to catch her breath in a little gasp.

'Do you like it?' Ellen whispered.

'It's exquisite,' Bel breathed, taking the piquant scent of female heat into her nostrils.

Ellen curled her fist in Bel's hair and released a long slow sigh. 'Then make me come, darling, and I'll do you.'

Bel cupped Ellen's bottom, pulled her close and buried her face deep in her massage therapist's wet gape, letting her intuition take over. After all, who knew how a woman wanted to be licked and sucked better than another woman?

Then, just when Bel was pretty sure Ellen was focused completely on her own pussy, she rearranged herself, wriggled free of her shoe and let it fall from the toilet roll dispenser to the floor with a clunk that made Bel jump. Bel marvelled at the woman's balance and flexibility as she shifted until her bare foot rested on the rim of the toilet seat, and her big toe wriggled its way back into Bel's pussy. Bel shoved three fingers home into Ellen's grasping cunt and licked and sucked her clit like it was a lollipop. She was pretty sure Ellen had managed to thrust more than her toe up inside her, pushing and shoving and stretching, every once in a while slipping out to press and stroke Bel's clit.

Outside the stall, other women came and went as the lunch crowd began to arrive. Toilets flushed, hand dryers ran, but none of that mattered. It was all peripheral to the probing and pushing and licking and shoving going on in the stall. They both came hard, Ellen nearly falling off her lone stiletto and Bel banging an elbow loudly on the insubstantial wall of the cubicle. The resulting waves of giggles and gasps were half-hidden in a flurry of sloppy, deep, laving kisses. Then, when the coast was clear, they tidied as best they could and hurried back to the table to eat their salad amid the lovely perfume of female heat.

* * *

'Darling, you're a million miles away, and you've barely touched your crème brulée.' Ellen ran a finger over the back of Bel's hand. 'Are you all right?'

'I'm fine. Really I am.' Bel forced a smile. 'It's just that, well, I need to know how to keep my fabulous gardener from taking another job.'

'The fabulous gardener who grows all the super veggies for you and the extra basil?'

Bel nodded. 'She's so wonderful and I adore her. I mean she's quiet and shy, but oh, you should see the lovely kitchen garden. Cook made the most fabulous baby aubergine curry the other night. Every single veg in the meal our sweet Francie had grown.'

Ellen stuck the tip of her finger in Bel's crème brulée and then licked it with a flick of her lovely pink tongue. 'Do you know why she's thinking about leaving?'

'I think it might be because she's lonely. I mean I've tried to get her to eat dinner occasionally with Dan and me. She's not just hired help, you know. She's an artist, like you are. But she won't. She doesn't go anywhere or do anything that I know of outside the garden.' Bel toyed with her spoon. 'I've tried to talk her into going with my sister and me for a girls' night out. I thought maybe we could introduce her to someone. My sister knows a lot of eligible men, but she says she's not a night owl. I don't know, Ellen, I'm at my wits' end, and I can't bear the thought of losing her.'

Ellen tongued her way around a forkful of chocolate mousse cheesecake. 'Maybe you need to be a little more sneaky about the whole situation, darling, and I may be able to help.' She leaned over the table, hazel eyes sparkling. 'My boyfriend has a friend who does –'

Bel nearly dropped her spoon. 'You have a boyfriend?'

'Yes, Doug. We live together. Is that a problem? I assumed you knew.'

'No! No problem at all. No problem.' Bel couldn't help the inward sigh of relief at knowing that Ellen had a boyfriend, and a fairly serious one at that. That made her situation seem even less like cheating. It was just a different sort of time out with a girlfriend. That's all. She pulled her attention back to what Ellen was saying.

'Anyway Doug has a friend who's, well, he's a starving artist, or was until he started moonlighting as an escort. He does so well that Doug's considering a bit of moonlighting himself, but never mind that.'

Bel blinked. 'You want me to hire a prostitute for Francie?'

'Not a prostitute, silly goose. Darrell is an escort. Oh, sex can be negotiated for extra money, but I figure what you really want for your girl is just someone to keep her company and make her feel good about herself, maybe boost her self-confidence a bit. If the sex happens, well, she need never know that it cost extra. She need never know anything, actually. Darrell is fabulous at making women feel good about themselves, and it doesn't matter if they're unattractive, Darrell knows how to make them feel like a supermodel. Your Francie, is she, you know, plain?'

'No. No, that's the thing, she's really very attractive. You don't suppose she's a lesbian, do you?'

Ellen leaned farther over the table and offered a wicked smile. 'Bel, darling, that would be the only way your Francie could resist Darrell. Shall I have Doug get in touch with him for you? I can even have him make all the arrangements if you'd like. That way she won't suspect you have anything to do with it, and we can just arrange payment once Darrell has confirmed.'

'You're sure she won't find out?'

'How could she? You haven't done anything, have you? And my boyfriend is the one making the arrangements. Might be just what Francie needs. What do you think?'

'If you're sure.' Bel gave Ellen's hand a hard squeeze. 'Go ahead, then. Anything to keep our Francie from leaving us.'

Chapter Seven

'How long have you been here?' Simon laid his portfolio on the table and sat down next to Dan in the pub where they'd agreed to meet. There were three empty pint glasses sitting in front of him and a fourth that was just about to join them. Simon had a sneaking suspicion there had been others. 'What's wrong?'

'It's Francie. She didn't show up today when we were supposed to meet.'

In spite of himself Simon felt an angry clench in his gut. It was hard to feel sympathetic.

'It's not like I don't deserve it,' Dan said, as though he read Simon's thoughts. 'I mean, what have I given her but pain? But I love her, Simon. I love her,' he whispered. For an embarrassing moment, Simon thought he was going to cry. He stared down at the cover of his portfolio to give the man a little private wallow in his much-deserved misery, something he didn't really want or need to see.

Simon remembered his conversation with Francie several days ago. She had asked him for a job. She said she had her reasons. Now he knew what they were, and even he had to admit that probably getting out of the situation would do her good. He wished he had something to offer her, but there was nothing, at least nothing suited to a woman with her talent and training. 'Is she gone?' he asked cautiously.

Dan shook his head. 'No. No, she came back from the nursery all right. Her car was in front of her flat when I came here, but she's not answering her mobile.'

'And you didn't go to her?'

'I couldn't, could I? If I'd gone to her that would have been it. I would have taken her right there. And then ...'

'And then you wouldn't have been faithful any more.' Simon said, but he was thinking that Dan was a coward. He would have gone after her in a heartbeat. He would have made damn sure she knew he appreciated what a woman she was. 'So ask for the bloody divorce, and get it over with,' he said, sounding every bit as unsympathetic as he felt.

'You don't understand, mate. My wife needs me right now. It's just not a good time. She's going through some kind of early midlife crisis. I don't know. She thinks she's old, she thinks she's ugly.' He waved a hand absently in the air. 'She's not. I mean if anything Bel gets prettier every day, but she doesn't see that, does she? She's eating strange foods, spending lots of time with her new-age, airy-fairy massage therapist, who's into all kinds of barmy rubbish.' He cocked his head slightly. 'Though I have to admit, it seems to be helping. Bel is getting better. But I just can't leave her at such a bad time. I can't leave until she's the old self-confident Bel again. Then … well, then I reckon she'll have another bloke lined up before the door slams behind me, and we'll all be happy.' He certainly didn't sound very happy. 'If we could just get through another month, maybe two, then I could see my way clear.' He turned to Simon so suddenly that Simon shoved his chair back with a screech on the slate floor. 'If you would just reconsider what we talked about earlier.'

'What? You mean the surrogate thing? Forget it. It doesn't take a lot of intelligence to see the trouble that would lead to.'

Dan downed the last of his pint, squared his shoulders and sat back. 'If you don't do this for me, I'll hire someone else to do the garden.'

Simon blew out a sharp breath. 'Are you blackmailing me?'

Dan didn't budge.

'Fine.' Simon stood and grabbed his portfolio from the table. 'Good luck with that, mate, the finding someone else, I mean.'

'Wait! Wait. I'm sorry. I didn't mean it.' Dan stood too, nearly knocking his chair over, and motioned Simon to sit back down. 'Of course I don't want anyone else to do the damned garden. It's just that, well, I can't lose Francie. I just can't. I'll pay you. No blackmail, no threat to your contract, just cash on top. However much you want, I'll pay.'

Simon eased back into his chair. 'I don't need your money, Dan. Look, whether or not I'm willing to do this ridiculous thing is irrelevant, really. If Francie loves you, then there's no way she'll settle for a substitute. Surely you must know that.'

The two sat in silence for a few minutes. The barmaid brought Dan another beer and took away the glasses. Sky Sports flashed silently on the big-screen TV. The after-work crowd began to clear, making room for the evening people.

'You could help me convince her.'

Simon sipped his beer and leaned over his portfolio towards Dan. 'So what if I did? What if I did help you convince her, and she did say yes? Are you really telling me you'd be all right watching me have sex with the woman you love, watching me pretend to be you?'

Dan held his gaze. 'If it would keep Francie here, if it

would keep her happy until I can ask Bel for the divorce, Simon, I'd do it. I'd do anything. Look, would you at least think about it? I mean, you said you think she's attractive, surely it wouldn't be a hardship for you, would it?'

In spite of himself, Simon couldn't block out thoughts of Francie sitting on the staging table in the greenhouse with her legs wrapped around him, her tongue making serious inroads into his mouth.

'Well? It wouldn't be, would it?'

Simon released a slow breath and shifted around the unwelcome stiffness now expanding to fill the front of his jeans. 'No. It wouldn't be a hardship.'

Dan heaved a desperate sigh. 'Then you'll consider it.'

'I didn't say that.'

'But you will. I know you will. I've always been able to count on you as a friend, Simon.'

Before Simon could bring up the fact that they hadn't seen each other in nearly ten years, Dan's phone bleeped with a text. He read it, squared his shoulders and pushed back from the table. 'It's Bel. I have to go. She's been going through a bad time lately, like I said. Can you meet tomorrow on the grounds? It'll help me a lot to see the plans in the daylight so I can get a picture of it in my head. I'm sure as hell not up for it tonight. Say around three?'

He was already calling a taxi and heading for the door before Simon had time to respond.

Simon took his time finishing his drink, while he attempted to look back through the drawings he'd made and scribble little notes in the margins. Attempting was about the best he could manage. Now that Dan had brought her up, it was impossible for him to think about anything but Francie. He had to admit, her gardening skills had him hard before he even got to the greenhouse and actually saw the woman in charge. But wow! Dan was insane not to just take her up against the wall, on the grass, in the greenhouse, every place he could. She was willing. The woman was sex in garden clogs. He'd only had her in his arms for a few minutes, but it was enough. It was enough for him to know that if he had fucked her, if the cook hadn't shown up when she did, she'd have made it well worth his while. He'd had several damn good wanks just thinking about it. And what he'd seen between her and Dan the other day under the oak tree had only added fuel to the fire. He wished he'd realised what was happening sooner, though, so he could have just left quietly and unnoticed. He hated it that he'd embarrassed her. Dan, not so much.

She had been decently dressed by the time he saw her, nothing to be embarrassed about really. Of course Dan jizzing all over the grass in front of him was a dead giveaway. He wondered what Francie had done to make the man shoot his wad so hard. He'd looked like the force of it would break him apart.

Suddenly Simon's cock felt too big for his jeans, expanding at a strange angle down in his boxers. Someone had turned up the volume on the telly. A raucous knot of women laughed loudly in one corner. No one was paying him any attention. He shifted in the chair and ran a hand down under the table to adjust himself. Even his touch through his jeans made him jerk and suck in his breath.

Francie! Christ, she might not be actually fucking the man, but she was still, for all practical purposes, Dan's mistress. This was not a situation Simon should even consider getting involved in. But he just wondered. He just wondered what would happen if he agreed to Dan's request. If Francie agreed. He wasn't particularly keen on Dan telling him what to do to Francie, what he'd do to her if he could. In fact he didn't give a rat's arse about Dan's lust.

But Francie's lust, well, that was another matter. He could easily imagine finishing what he'd started there in the greenhouse several days ago. Or maybe Dan would have them meet in the remote area set aside for the Renaissance garden. The vision in his mind was so vivid that he could almost smell her, like he'd smelled her in the greenhouse, smelled the scent of a woman, sweaty and warm and open. In the remote quiet of the Renaissance garden, he could imagine pushing her down on the grass. It would be easy enough to slip up that lovely little skirt she wore and run his hand down inside her panties where she would be wet and sticky and needing the touch of a man.

By the time Dan had his cock out in his hand, Simon, in his mind's eye, would have stealthily, quietly tweaked her, rubbed her, caressed her. Simon would have already given her more than she had ever got from Dan. And she would be making little birdlike moans and whimpers, as he pulled off her knickers and opened her legs. Then he'd bury his face in her pussy. He wouldn't make her wait for it. He'd do what he could to make up for all the times that she'd only got a wank while Dan went home to fuck his wife. And God, with the delicious way she smelled, he could only imagine how she must taste.

One of the women in the corner of the pub let out a shriek of laughter, and the others immediately joined in, jarring him back from his fantasy. He was horrified to find himself rocking and shifting in his chair, his hand still resting, rather rudely, on his fly. He stood up and made sure his portfolio strategically covered the bulge that had him walking like he had something rammed up his arse. He needed to get to his car. There he could take care of himself in private. He'd have to do something. Thoughts of burying his face in Francie's cunt had him too far gone to just ignore it.

But the car park was full of people with fags in one hand and pints in the other. And with the long summer hours of daylight, even in his car he'd feel exposed. He cursed briefly, belted himself in and headed out on to the road. He wasn't actually conscious of where he was driving. His head was too full of Francie, and of Dan's proposition. But somehow he ended up on the road at the back of Dan's property. It was far enough away from the house that he couldn't see anything, and it was private. It was as close to home as he was likely to manage without some relief first.

'Shit,' he said out loud into the silence. 'I feel like a goddamned stalker.' He pushed the seat back as far as it would go and reclined it, then he opened his fly and uttered a pathetic whimper at the feel of his sensitive heft. Jesus, this whole situation was really doing a number on him, and yet he couldn't stop thinking about it now that Dan had made the offer.

Almost as though he had pushed the pause button in his head, he picked up where he had left off at the pub, with his face buried between Francie's delectable folds. He could imagine the powerful muscles in her thighs quivering with control as she struggled not to close her legs around his face. But he wouldn't let her go, he would keep the pressure up until she bucked under him and convulsed, and he'd feel her whole pussy quiver as she came. He would give her that gift before he ever mounted her, the gift she'd been denied all this time with Dan. And as she caught her breath, one hand would be curled tightly in his hair, holding him to her, but with the other she would be playing with her breasts. She had been braless both times he'd seen her. Oh, he definitely hadn't missed that. He hadn't missed the feel of tight nipples pressing through thin summer fabric like they'd drill their way right on in through his T-shirt, maybe even on through his chest.

With a tight grunt, he scooped his balls free from his boxers and cupped and kneaded, stifling a curse and pressing his thumb to the head of his cock, surprised at just how much muscle memory was there when he recalled the feel of her tight nipples, the feel of the woman in his arms. It didn't seem to matter that it had only been fleeting.

When he was sure he wasn't going to spurt all over himself, he began to stroke and tug again. In his mind's eye, he worked his way up Francie's delicious body until he could service those lovely tits for her. Oh fuck, how he'd service her nipples, her delicious high, taut nipples! He could almost feel them. And her smell, her smell would be all over him. He'd be wet with her scent, with her juices, as he fumbled to free his cock, as she opened her legs to him. Simon would finger open Francie's swollen pussy lips, while Dan's breathless grunts, along with the slap, slap, slap of his wanking, furnished the soundtrack. In his mind's eye, Simon would then slide home, giving her something she'd not had since Dan wormed his way into her life, giving her hard hungry cock, cock just as needy as she was. And God, she would be deep and tight, and she would grip him until it took every ounce of his control to keep from spilling.

In the real world, efforts to keep from spilling were failing miserably. In a move none too graceful, a move that he barely managed, he jerked open the car door and swung his legs out just as his cock convulsed hard, and he exploded on to the gravel, barely missing the edge of the door with his wad.

When he'd got his breath back, he cleaned himself up then headed home. The image of Francie lying in his arms on the grass, both of them completely sated, lingered in his head. Strangely, Dan was not included in the afterglow.

Chapter Eight

'Thanks, Francie, darling. You're a star,' Bel called over her shoulder, nearly running into Simon on her way out of the greenhouse with a basket of veg and two more basil plants.

He lightly stepped out of her way, barely avoiding some baby spinach growing near the edge of the stone path.

'Oh dear, I should look where I'm going. I'm so sorry.' She looked up at him and offered him a knowing smile. 'You must be Darrell.' She raised a finger to her lips, then glanced over her shoulder towards Francie. 'But I never saw you.' She winked and tiptoed away before he could correct her.

Simon was the last person Francie wanted to face after her enormous success at making a fool of herself every time they saw each other. But she was trapped, standing wet-handed over a sudsy sink full of terracotta pots. He didn't seem to notice her captured-rabbit look. He offered her a smile that was surprisingly warm considering their previous encounters. She turned back to the sink so he wouldn't see her face, so she wouldn't have to meet his gaze.

'Was that Bel?' he asked.

'In the basil-eating flesh.' She tried to keep her voice calm and light.

'Other than devouring all your basil, she seems like a nice person.'

'Oh, she is. She's lovely. She'd do anything for me and I …' Her voice drifted off. She bit her lip and focused on her work, scrubbing at the pots like her life depended on it.

He politely pretended not to notice the near outbreak of emotions. 'Did she just call me Darrell? Wonder what that was all about.'

'No idea. She's usually very good with names. Dan's up at the house, I think.' The butterflies leaped in her stomach. She wished he would just leave her alone with her embarrassment.

But he didn't. He moved to stand behind her, too close for comfort. She swore she could feel his hot breath on the back of her neck. 'I'm not actually here to see Dan. I came to see you.'

'Me?' A pot slipped from her nervous fingers and gave her a good splashing. She jumped back and found herself pressed against a solid wall of maleness, and she was suddenly paralysed with the feel of him, with the rise and fall of him, with the clean male sweat smell of him as he reached around her for the towel that lay on the shelf next to the sink.

'Yes, you. Assuming you're still interested in working somewhere other than here, that is.' She took the towel from him and turned to face him, forcing herself to look up into his lovely grey eyes. He continued. 'I think I understand a little better, now, why you want to work elsewhere.'

She blushed hard and side-stepped the near embrace of him, wiping her neck and cleavage self-consciously. Her mouth suddenly felt cotton-dry. 'About the other day —' she forced a grunt of pained laughter '— and the time before that. I'm sorry —'

'It's not a full-time job, but it's a start.' His interruption felt like an act of sheer kindness. 'Though I think it might develop into something a whole lot more, something rather exciting, actually, if you're as good as I think you are. Oh, it won't get you away from here immediately, but I think it might interest you enough, keep you busy enough to, you know —' he offered her a broad-shouldered shrug '— get your mind off things.'

She wiped at her eyes frantically, not wanting to cry in front of him again, not wanting him to think less of her than he surely already did. She swallowed the tight lump in her throat. 'I haven't been with him since, well, since you saw, but I still have to work.' She looked around her at the greenhouse and out over the veg patch and the raised beds beyond. 'It was actually Bel who hired me, and I owe her at least a few fucking basil plants, don't I?'

'It's none of my business, Francie,' he said. 'People make mistakes. Things happen.'

In spite of her best effort, her lip quivered, and her vision misted. 'If he comes to me, if he even makes the slightest attempt at an apology, which I know he will, then I won't be able to turn him away. I won't.'

He took a step closer. 'Do you want to? Turn him away, I mean.'

She shook her head and wiped at her eyes again. 'I don't know what I want. I love him, but then I look around me at what we have, which isn't much, and what little we do have is stolen from her.' She nodded to where Bel had disappeared down the path. 'And I like her. She's a good person. She doesn't deserve any of this.'

'And you do?' He took her by the shoulders and shook her very gently until she looked up and met his gaze again. And there he was, that earnest face, those startling eyes, the full, parted lips. His touch was like fire on her arms. Her stomach did a somersault, and things farther south went all liquid and soft.

'There you are, Francie.'

They jumped apart as Dan burst into the greenhouse and, when he saw the two of them together, for the briefest of seconds everything froze. Then he reached behind him and slowly closed the greenhouse door. 'I wasn't expecting to see you here, Simon, but I'm very glad you are.' His face broke into a broad smile, and he stepped forward. 'Francie, darling, Simon is my gift to you, if you'll accept.'

'What?' both Francie and Simon said at the same time.

'Oh, this is so exciting!' Dan came to stand next to the two and laid a hand on Simon's shoulder, but was careful not to touch Francie. 'I knew you'd come around, Simon.'

'But I didn't. I haven't,' Simon said, stepping away from Francie.

Dan wasn't listening. 'Francie, darling, I know how hard it is for you, with us not able to really be with each other. I promise that'll end soon, and we can be together properly. But in the meantime, it's not right me having Bel and you having no one. So I've come up with a solution for us. Simon will be my surrogate.'

'What?' Francie had pushed herself back against the sink as far as she could. Her heart raced in her throat and her face felt like it would burst into flame. 'You want me to … You want us to …' She nodded towards Simon, then she glared up at him. 'Is this why you're here?'

81

But before Simon could do more than make a couple of fish gasps, Dan ploughed on. 'Oh, don't you see, darling, it's so perfect. If I can't be with you, if I can't give you what I know you so desperately need, then who better to help us both out than my dearest, most trusted friend, Simon?'

'He's a landscaper. He's hired help just like I am.' She sounded a lot more hysterical than she meant to. What she wanted to sound was outraged. What she wanted to sound was incensed.

'No, sweetheart, no. Simon and I are old friends. We went to uni together. We spent a wild summer in Italy together. Darling, I'd trust Simon with my life.' He shot Simon a meaningful glance, then his gaze came to rest on her. 'I'd trust him with the person in my life I value most, the one I most want to make happy.' He caught his breath, and his face softened. 'Please, darling. This is a gift, something I can do for you. You can pretend he's me. I can make love to you through Simon, and you, anything you've wanted to do to me you can do to him.'

'Anything?' She spoke through the racing of her heart, which felt like it would jump right out of her mouth.

'Yes, anything, darling. Anything.'

'Good.' Before she had time to consider what she was doing, she slapped Simon hard, hard enough that he recoiled. Both men gasped, and her hand stung like fire. But she ignored the pain, squared her shoulders and looked Simon right in his now watering grey eyes. 'Then you can give him that for me.'

To her total surprise, Simon did exactly as she said. He walked over to Dan and slapped him, slapped him hard enough to knock Dan up against the staging table, slapped him hard enough to draw blood where a tooth cut his lip.

The electric silence that followed was interrupted only by the heavy breathing of all three. The two men glared at each other for a moment, sizing one another up. Trembling all over, Francie grabbed the edge of the sink for support, just as Simon turned his back on Dan and came to stand in front of her. He stood so close his breath ruffled the hair that had come loose from the clasp she wore it up in, so close that the rise and fall of his chest beneath his T-shirt was impossible to ignore, so close the heat rising from his body felt magnetic.

'Does that about sum it up?' he asked.

For a second, she thought she might cry. But instead, she threw her arms around his neck and kissed him. She kissed him as hard as she had slapped him, like she wanted to eat him up, like she wanted to crawl up inside his warmth. And he kissed her back. Jesus, how he kissed her back! He kissed and nipped the hollow of her throat around to the sensitive place below her ear, then he whispered in between efforts to breathe. 'If you want me to stop, tell me now before it's too late.'

'Don't you dare, don't you dare, don't you dare,' she gasped over and over again, guiding his hand to the knot tied below her right breast that held her wraparound dress closed.

He yanked it hard, then he pushed the dress until it slid from her shoulders and pooled on the floor around her gardening clogs. Somewhere on the periphery of her mind she heard Dan's fly unzip, a sound she'd grown used to over the past few months, a sound that constantly taunted her with everything she could see yet never touch.

But there were other things to focus on today. Simon kissed his way down her sternum and cupped her breasts, cupped them and kneaded them until her nipples strained against the calluses of his stroking fingers. Then his mouth took over. What her breasts lacked in size, they made up for in sensitivity, and her whole body thrummed as he suckled and bit, nibbled and licked.

'That's it, Simon, kiss her breasts,' Dan grunted. 'Oh God, bury your face in them, revel in them. How I've fantasised about doing just that.'

From the corner of her eye, Francie could see Dan stroking his cock, but it was little more than a slight distraction. Simon's fingers slipped into the top of her panties and began to caress her tight curls. Her body tensed, then went liquid as his fingers worried their way down over the nub of her clit and in between her swollen lips.

'Is she wet?' Dan asked.

Simon nodded, still suckling a heavy nipple. 'And she's hard.' He spoke against her breast, raking the rough pad of his thumb across her clit, making her whimper out loud. He caught her just as her knees gave from under her and lifted her effortlessly on to the staging table, elbowing a stack of wet seedling trays out of the way. Then he grabbed her knickers on either side, peeled them off and let them drop to the floor. She could feel the warm air in the greenhouse against her bare cunt.

'Mmmm, I can smell how horny she is,' Dan said, moving to stand behind Simon so he could get a better view. 'Taste her, Simon. She must taste as good as she smells.'

But Simon wasn't really paying any attention to Dan. He worked his way up the inside of one thigh, pushing her open as he went. He nipped her soft inner flesh until the sounds coming from her throat became less human, more feral, until the grinding of her arse against the hard wood of the table would no doubt leave bruises. And all the while her pussy pouted and gripped and wet the table beneath.

When she could take the torturous teasing of his mouth no longer, she grabbed him by the hair and pulled his face to her pussy. He not only yielded to her demand but cupped her buttocks in his large hands and pulled her to him, nuzzling intimately into her depths, as though he would eat his way clear into the centre of her.

The garden clogs dropped to the floor with a loud ka-thunk. She lifted both feet to his shoulders, pressing still harder, driving her cunt up closer against his face. He groaned and yanked her still closer, his hands bruising her butt.

'Oh God! That's wonderful, that's amazing,' Dan breathed. 'It feels so good, doesn't it, Francie? It's just what you need, isn't it, darling?'

With a deep raking of his tongue that began at her perineum and ended with a hard suckling nip of her clit, Simon sent Francie growling and bucking into orgasm. Jesus, she had forgotten what it felt like when someone other than herself did the honours.

'That's it, sweetheart, come for me,' Dan cooed.

'I'm not coming for you, damn it!' she gasped. 'I'm coming for me.' Then she sat up and clawed at the fly of Simon's jeans. 'Take them off. Now! I want you inside me.'

She barely had the words out of her mouth before Simon's trousers and boxers were down around his hips and the substantial cock she'd admired through his jeans only a few days ago was free. She reached between her legs and grabbed him. He gasped, as she wriggled and manoeuvred until the head of his cock was flush against her open pout. He let her position herself and, when she was ready, he pushed in with a grunt.

It hurt. And it felt good all at the same time. God, it had been so long. And Simon seemed to know exactly how much pain was a good thing, and what he was doing was a very good thing indeed.

'Do you want to see?' he gasped. 'Do you want to see what it looks like? What we look like?'

'Yes,' Dan murmured, and he moved in closer, tugging on his cock like there was no tomorrow. But Simon wasn't talking to him. Simon's eyes were locked on Francie's as she pushed up on her elbows to see what it looked like down there where they were joined, where Simon was thrusting up inside her. Then she wrapped her legs around his hips and pushed up to meet him, feeling everything grasp. The muscles of his abdomen tensed with each thrust. The whole world tightened around them, and Francie forgot how to breathe.

'Oh God, oh fuck, oh sweet Jesus,' Dan repeated, like a breathless mantra.

Simon looked like he'd turned to stone. He was hard all over. Only his hips kept thrusting, harder and deeper and tighter. Then his gaze caught hers. 'Are you ready?' he gasped. She gave him a hint of a nod, all she could manage at the moment. Then he pulled her up to him, wrapped his arms around her and held her tight up against him, like she was his flesh, like she was his breath, like she was his own body, and he knew exactly how to love her. All the while Dan chanted, 'Oh God, oh fuck, oh Christ.' Then he came, catching his wad in a handkerchief he had at some point extricated from his pocket.

'Are you ready?' Simon whispered again, next to her ear.

She was too far gone to speak. She only held him tighter and uttered a whimper. Then he moved just right so that the constant stroking and rubbing of his pubic bone against her clit pressed a little deeper, a little harder, and she tumbled over the edge, her arms and legs wrapped around him, her face buried in his nape. He was a split second behind her.

Dan was suddenly at their side, his trousers still down below his arse, his hand gripping Francie's. 'That's it, my sweet Francie, what you need, what you deserve. Yes, my darling. Take it. It's for you. All I want is to see your pleasure.'

Then it all happened at once. Dan's cell phone rang. A stack of terracotta pots tumbled off the end of the table and shattered on the floor with a loud crash, and Simon stepped back looking like a man who had just woken up from a dream.

'I have to go,' he said, breathlessly. None too gently, he shoved his heavy equipment back into his jeans. Then he turned and fled. Dan was on the phone with Bel. Francie slid into her dress and made an exit by the back door before he could stop her.

Chapter Nine

Please don't be angry, Francie, but let me give you this gift. It's what I can give you, all I can give you right now. Please accept it, tell me you're OK with it. Simon's a good man. He would never betray us. Let Simon be your comfort, let him satisfy your needs for a little while, my love. And when the time comes, as soon as I'm able, I'll be the one in your arms.

Francie read the email over and over again until the words became an unfocused jumble on the page, and still she read them. The email wasn't signed. That would be risky. But Dan had never emailed her at all before. It was a bold step forward for him.

She wanted to be angry and outraged. She wanted to tell both him and Simon to fuck off. No! What she wanted was to just leave. Let them wonder where she was. No! What she wanted was ... What she wanted was to have Simon between her legs again while Dan watched and wanked. That was what she wanted. That was the truth of it.

As lovely and sweet as the email was, in truth nothing that had ever happened to her was as hot as Simon fucking her while Dan watched and masturbated. Strange, but it felt so much less like she was cheating, so much less like she was betraying poor Bel. It felt so much more like hot kink, something she would never have done anywhere but in her fantasies, and yet she had instigated it. She had practically jumped all over Simon. And she wanted to do it again.

She hit reply on Dan's email and wrote:

Thank you for your gift. I accept it. I'm OK with it.

Then she sent it.

* * *

'You're here.'

Francie turned to find Simon standing in the doorway of the greenhouse, his gorgeous grey gaze locked on her in a way that made her feel suddenly giddy. 'I wasn't sure you'd be all right with it, with what happened.' He suddenly seemed shy, looking down at his shoes, shifting from foot to foot. 'I wasn't sure I'd be all right with it, actually, but here I am.' He met her gaze again and offered a smile that made her insides somersault.

'You're early.' Her voice sounded thin, nervous. She kept her hands busy with the tomato plant she was pruning. It kept them from shaking.

'I didn't get a chance to give you this last time.' He laid a piece of paper on the staging table. 'I didn't know your email address or I would have emailed it.'

'What is it?' She wiped her hands on her dress tail and came to his side.

'It's an address and phone number. A woman I built a mediaeval maze for a couple of years ago wants a potager. I told her that decorative vegetable gardens aren't exactly my forte. I mean I could do a little research and build one for her, but I told her I knew someone who could design her the most amazing potager in the history of potagers.' He frowned at the blank look she offered him. 'The job? Remember? What we were talking about before Dan showed up. You did say you had some design experience, right?'

'Really? You were serious about the job?'

'Of course I was serious. What did you think?'

Blushing hard, she picked up the paper and concentrated on it, avoiding his gaze. 'I thought you were here because ...'

He curled a finger beneath her chin and forced her to look into his eyes. 'I intended to tell Dan no.' He ran a rough thumb across her lower lip, and her insides erupted in fireworks. 'It's not that I didn't want you. It's just that, well, the way it happened was not the way I had fantasised our coming together. Besides, I didn't think you'd say yes.'

'I wouldn't have,' she said. That he had actually fantasised about them coming together pleased her more than she could say.

He caught his breath and stepped back, as though he suddenly remembered where he was. He nodded towards the paper. 'I know Lavinia Haskins, and I know her property. I've done a lot of work for her. She's very accommodating where her gardens are concerned, willing to listen to good advice. I'll go with you the first time you meet her, to introduce you and to show you around the property. I know what little quirks and problems you'll face with her garden. It's clay, at least the part you'll be dealing with. And it's got a quirky aspect, but I've learned a few secrets while working for her that'll help you out a little. You do want to do this, don't you?'

'Yes, I do. It's time. It's definitely time.' She tucked the paper into her seed box and locked it back down in the cupboard below the staging table, then she looked up at him. 'I think we should probably go.'

He offered her a nervous smile, then held out his arm for her. 'Shall we see what Dan has in store for us, then?'

She took his arm and they walked side by side down

to the stream. 'I know where Dan wants us to meet him,' Simon said. 'I've been sketching it. It's the place where he wants to build the grotto, a place where the stream's a little deeper, a little calmer.'

'I know the spot,' Francie said. 'It's one of my favourites.'

Sure enough, Dan was waiting for them there, a blanket spread on the grass next to the water. He nodded for them to sit. For a long moment he looked quietly from one of them to the other, and just as the silence got uncomfortable, he took a deep breath and spoke.

'You were both very naughty the last time we were together, weren't you?'

In spite of herself, Francie felt a wave of guilt that she had enjoyed Simon so much. She was just about to get defensive when Dan offered a wicked smile and continued. 'You just did what you wanted, didn't you?'

The two looked at each other, speechless, then looked back at him.

'Oh, it was OK for our first time together, since it really wasn't planned, and we really didn't know what to expect from our little adventure. But now that we've all seen how well it can work, now that we all know it's something that'll be good for all of us, I think it's time I remind you, Simon, that you're my surrogate. In our future trysts, you'll do what I ask you to. Are we clear?'

Simon bristled, but said nothing.

'And Francie, I would ask that you think of Simon as me, that you ask him to do what you would like me to do to you if I could. Do to him what you would to me.' He chuckled softly and rubbed his jaw. 'Mind you I'm hoping that you've worked most of the violence out of your system by now. Don't know how much more my jaw can take.'

Neither Simon nor Francie laughed. Francie could feel the tension in Simon's shoulders. She feared he might be so angry that he would leave without her having him inside her again. The thought was almost unbearable.

'OK, then, shall we begin?' It pissed her off that Dan sounded so much like he was the chairman of the board, and they were only his employees, though that was the uncomfortable truth of the matter. And yet at the same time it was a bit of a turn-on. 'Simon, kiss her. Take her into your arms and kiss her because that's what I'd do if I had just met her here, if I were just getting ready to make love to her. If I were free.'

Simon, sitting on the blanket next to her, turned slightly. She could see the hammering of his pulse in his throat, the colour climbing up his cheeks. His large hand cupped her jaw and he lifted her chin, holding her gaze with eyes that she wanted desperately to be able to read right now, eyes that she wanted to be able to reassure that Dan's arrogance was nothing personal, just a male thing. Then Simon's lips settled on hers, warm and parted, his breath tingled against her mouth, his tongue flicked

94

stealthily between her teeth in search of hers. He swallowed the sigh she released, the sigh laced with the last three days of fear that this, this coming together again, might not happen.

Dan sighed along with them and came closer, joining them on the blanket. 'You like that, don't you, darling? Of course you do. Who doesn't like a good snogging?' Then he turned his attention to Simon.

'Tell me what she feels like. Tell me, Simon. You don't know how I've dreamed about the feel of her.'

'She's soft.' Simon spoke against her mouth. His hand moved beneath her hair to cradle her head 'And warm.' His tongue flicked over hers. 'And she tastes like honey and heat and summer. She tastes better than anything.'

Dan's groan was almost painful. 'Like I imagined, like I imagined. And her breasts, Simon, her breasts are so lovely. You know, she never wears a bra. That makes me so damned horny. I bet it does you too, doesn't it? Open her top so we can see her breasts. Yes, that's it,' he breathed, as Simon fumbled to open the buttons at the top of her dress. Francie couldn't help noticing that his hands were trembling with nerves. But so were hers.

He pushed the dress off her shoulders, lifted her breasts free, and she arched and stretched into his caress.

'Oh God, yes. So lovely, so lovely,' Dan whispered. He shifted on the blanket and released his cock from his fly. 'You must be about to burst, Simon. I know I am.

Take your cock out. Go on. That's what I would do. No, wait. Francie, do it for him. Go on. Open his fly and free his cock.'

And suddenly her trembling was almost uncontrollable. Here she was opening the fly of the man who had invaded her dreams, dreams she figured were probably just revenge dreams. But this wasn't a dream, and it was Dan asking her to do it. Her pussy felt warm and heavy, swelling between her legs with an agenda that wasn't concerned about who had asked her to do what, but concerned only with the end result.

Simon leaned back on the blanket, watching her from beneath heavy lids, and when she fumbled with hands made clumsy by nerves and desire, he steadied her. 'It's all right, Francie,' he whispered. 'It's all right. I'm all right with this.'

'Will you be that nervous with me, our first time, Francie, darling?' Dan said. 'I would be at least that nervous with you.'

She lost track of what Dan was saying as she gripped the heft of Simon's cock, felt his breath catch, felt his hand tighten over hers as he lifted his arse and shoved at his jeans and boxers until he was free, exquisitely, beautifully free in her hand. And suddenly she couldn't breathe for want of him.

'Take him in your mouth, Francie,' she heard Dan say from a long way off.

And she did, she took the weight of him into her mouth, greedily, hungrily, until she nearly gagged herself. She felt the strangled rake of his breath, felt his fingers curl in her hair and press down along her ear. 'Ah, God,' he murmured.

'It's good, isn't it, Simon? Exquisite, being in her mouth, feeling her tongue against the underside of your cock. You feel that, don't you Simon? Don't you?'

Simon didn't speak, only nodded, lifting his arse and lowering it, lifting and lowering to meet her.

'Take off her panties, Simon. Feel how wet she is, how swollen. Then touch her down there, play with her, make her come on your fingers. Do it for me.'

She rearranged herself so that Simon could ease her panties down over her hips while she continued to lick and suck. Then she kicked them free. In her peripheral vision, she saw Dan move on the blanket, and she opened her legs wide, knowing that he wanted to look at her.

'Touch her, Simon.' Dan's voice was hoarse, tight in his throat. 'Touch her little pussy for me. My God, she's so wet and slick, and her lips are all pearled with her juices and swollen. She could take your cock now, Simon. Would you like that? I know you would.'

Still grinding and shifting against her mouth, Simon slid his hand down between the two of them, over her pubic curls, to tweak the nub of her clit before he slid two fingers deep into her cunt, and she heard Dan sigh.

'Oh God, Simon. She must feel better than anything.'

Simon matched the rhythmic thrusts of his fingers to the up-and-down bobbing of her head on his cock, then he began to circle his thumb around and up and over the hard pebble of her clit until she bore down and raked against him, until she could feel herself wetting his hand, until she could feel her juices dripping over his palm.

'Oh Jesus, I've never seen anything more exquisite,' Dan gasped.

And Simon knew secrets; he knew the hard press and circle of two fingers against her G-spot would send her gushing and convulsing, shivers of heat curling up her spine. She pulled away from his cock, fearing that in her tremors of lust she might hurt him. With his fingers still tight in her hair, he pulled her to his mouth and kissed her hard while she gushed and quivered.

'Jesus,' Dan whispered. 'Jesus, darling, you're beautiful when you're coming so hard. I want so badly to be inside you. Simon, do you want to be inside her now? I know you do. You must hardly be able to contain yourself. Would you like that, Francie? Would you like to sit on Simon's hard cock, have him push it right up into your wet little hole?'

Francie could only murmur and nod with Simon's mouth pressed against hers, his tongue teasing her tongue. But she need do no more. Simon pulled her close to him and lifted her bottom, settling her on to his lap with a leg on either side of him. Then he fingered her open and impaled her inch by inch until she felt fuller than full, until her muscles tightened and gripped and pulsated around the whole substantial length of him.

Simon sucked a breath between his teeth at her tight squeeze, and Dan sighed. 'Oh, that must feel so exquisite, being up inside our Francie's delicious cunt. Tell me. Tell me, Simon, how does it feel?'

'Tight. Wet. So soft and warm.' Simon began to thrust beneath her and she wrapped her legs around him. 'Like I never want to stop,' he breathed.

Dan moved close, so close Francie could practically feel the heat of him. She could feel his breath coming in tight, desperate pulls. She could hear the hard slap, slap of his own efforts for some relief.

'That's it, my lovely Francie. That's it, darling, make him come, make Simon come the way you would make me come, if I were up inside you driving my cock deep into your dirty little cunt. Simon would like that, I know he would.'

Simon forced her back on the grass and drove into her like he was possessed, like the need was beyond urgent, like he knew that she couldn't wait much longer either. As they both tipped over the edge together, she realised that yes, she had been waiting, she had been waiting to go with him, to feel him come when she did. A split second later, panting desperately, Dan shot his wad on to the grass next to them.

Then they all collapsed in a heap. Simon shifted so his weight wasn't on top of Francie, but his cock was still nestled in her pussy. Dan settled in as close as he could get without touching her, close enough that she could feel his breath against her skin. Then, very lightly, he rested his hand on her shoulder. 'There, my darling. There, my sweet Francie. That was so good. It was so good for you, wasn't it?'

She sighed and nodded, but found it impossible to speak, locked in the heat of Simon's possessive gaze.

Chapter Ten

'By the way, sweetie –' Bel made a lazy circle around Ellen's erect nipple with the very tip of her French-manicured nail '– Darrell is totally delicious. I've seen him twice now, and I think it's working. Francie certainly seems a lot more perky. And having him dress like a gardener is brilliant. I doubt anything he could do to her between the sheets would impress her more than him knowing his way around a compost heap.'

Ellen's giggle nearly toppled her off the massage table they were both crowded on to. 'I knew that Darrell did his homework, but wow! I'd say it's no wonder he's in such high demand. And a fast study too. I didn't even know that Doug had made the arrangements yet. Well, never mind. Glad it's working.'

Bel heaved a breathy sigh and slipped off the table. 'Sadly, we need to go, darling. It's getting late. We don't want to keep poor Barton waiting, do we?'

The two women dressed and tidied. They didn't shower. It had become their routine in the short time they'd been seeing each other to ride home in the limo together. The flat Ellen lived in wasn't that much out of the way. Not that it mattered. Dan never noticed when Bel got home. She and Ellen always had a naughty ride to Ellen's apartment, then Bel showered when she got home. It gave her a chance to enjoy the scent of their shared pleasure just a little longer.

Bel had just pushed Ellen into the limo ahead of her and made a bull's-eye grab for her tight bottom beneath her flip skirt before both women froze, mid-giggle, at the sight of Dan sitting opposite them peeking over the top of the *Financial Times*.

They quickly seated themselves and shot each other a caught-in-the-act glance.

'Dan, darling, I hadn't expected you here,' Bel finally managed.

'Obviously,' he said, looking from one woman to the other. Then he settled his attention on the masseuse. 'Ellen.' He nodded his greeting as the limo pulled out of the car park, then he returned his attention to Bel. 'Sorry to interrupt your … girl time, but I had Barton pick me up from the office on his way. The meeting ended early, and it seemed an efficient use of his time.'

'Efficient indeed, dear.' Bel forced a smile and brazenly rested her hand on Ellen's knee. 'We'll have dinner together then after all. What a lovely surprise.'

'Yes, lovely.' He returned his attention to his paper.

Bel felt like she'd eaten ground glass. Was he really that stupid, or did he just not care? Humiliation burned up through her chest, and she might have cried if Ellen hadn't curled her fingers around Bel's hand and gently massaged her knuckles with her thumb. Her touch was comforting, somehow reassuring, and Bell rested her head on Ellen's shoulder. The paper trembled slightly, then Dan turned the page, nearly ripping it out in his effort. And in spite of herself, Bel felt a sense of relief. A least it mattered enough to make him angry. Anger was at least something. She was sick to death of his indifference.

With Dan ensconced all prickly and cold behind his newspaper, the drive to Ellen's, which was usually over way too soon, seemed interminable. When the limo finally stopped at Ellen's flat, Bel's insides were roiling that Dan could be such a total prick. She pulled her masseuse into a tight hug, then thought better of it, and gave her a hard kiss on the mouth, hard enough for them both to pull away breathless.

'I'll see you next time,' Ellen whispered. Then she offered Dan a curt nod, which he acknowledged with a pained smile and a grunt.

When the door shut behind her and the limo pulled away from the curb, Dan snapped the paper shut. For a long second he glared at his wife. But she glared right back, refusing to squirm. At last he spoke. 'You smell like cunt.'

She nodded. 'I suppose I do after having licked out Ellen's pussy.'

The tight muscles along his jaw bone spasmed. 'Are you having a laugh?'

She folded her arms across her chest. 'Do I look like I'm having a laugh?'

'You had sex with her?'

She faltered. 'Well, it's not really sex, is it? I mean, we're both women.'

'Jesus! You're having sex with your massage therapist. Am I not enough for you?'

'Enough for me?' The laugh that erupted from her throat felt rough, abrasive. 'How the hell would I know if you're enough for me, Dan, when you never do more than your duty, and even then you act like you're doing me a favour.'

'My duty?' He shoved the paper off his lap and, for the first time, she noticed he was hard enough to threaten the integrity of his trousers. The thought barely registered before he moved across the seat, curled one hand into her hair and jerked her into a kiss that she was sure would leave her lips bruised. His fly was open, and he had her down on the seat, literally ripping off the sopping remains of her thong, shoving his fingers into her pussy, still wet from her rendezvous with Ellen. 'Duty's a two-way street, Bel, and it's a fucking boring word, isn't it?' He gave her clit a rough pinch with his thumb and forefinger, then shoved into her so hard it took her breath away. With the first thrust he bit her neck until she yelped and her eyes watered, all the while fighting and squirming beneath him. Well, at least she started out fighting, scratching and punching. But then he grabbed her arms and pinned them above her head in one large hand.

'You want more than me doing my duty, I'll give you more. How much more do you want?' He emphasised the question with a devastating thrust, his breath coming fast and heavy against her face.

She bit his cheek, hard. 'I want all of you, goddamn it! Why the fuck do you think I married you?'

Then there was no more talking. She wrapped her legs around him and dug her heels into his kidneys. He pulled her deep into his embrace like she was a rag doll, and they fucked in hard, brutal thrusts. They fucked until her eyes watered from the harsh, breathtaking impact. At least, that's why she told herself her eyes were watering. He came in a storm surge, and her orgasm shattered through her like crystal against stone. Only when the convulsions had dissipated did they realise the limo had stopped moving and the driver had discreetly left them to it.

Dan zipped his fly with an angry tug, then yanked her out of the limo so hard she feared he'd dislocate her shoulder. 'I never knew you were such a filthy bitch,' he muttered into her ear, offering the limo driver a tight smile that he must have known would never pass for normal.

'I never knew it was filthy bitches you liked,' she growled under her breath. 'I thought you liked it all nice and clean and sanitised.'

With his arm tightly around her, he half guided her, half dragged her into the house, into the kitchen, where he shoved her up against the refrigerator, rattling the contents. 'I like my fucking bathroom clean and sanitised, not my wife.' He grabbed her hair and kissed her like he'd swallow her whole, kissed her until she struggled to breathe. Then he lifted her, with her back against the cool metal of the refrigerator, and shoved into her again. She was amazed that he was hard already. They hadn't had back-to-back sex since their early days of marriage, but he was like a battering ram. He ripped open her blouse. Buttons flew, fabric tore, as he forced her breasts up over her plunge bra to be brutalised by his hungry hands. It hurt. And it made her hotter than anything she'd ever felt. 'Ellen can't do this, can she?' he said, thrusting up hard inside her.

She shoved her hands up under his shirt, clawed at his shoulders and thrust back just as hard. 'I don't want

Ellen to do that. I fucking want you to do that.' He had her coming again, no doubt drenching the front of his always pristine trousers in her flood, and he wasn't far behind her. Then he lifted her into his arms and carried her upstairs to their big bed.

* * *

The bedding was a shambles, tangled and sweaty, and the remains of the dinner tray they'd had delivered to their suite were strung across the room, along with an empty wine bottle. The smell of sex offered a pungent, heated bass note to the ambient fragrance. 'Be honest, you like the smell of Ellen on me, don't you?' Bel asked as Dan buried his face between her breasts, kneading them and thumbing her nipples.

'Mmm. Nothing quite as nice as the smell of pussy,' he breathed. 'She must have had her pussy all over you to leave her scent on your tits.'

'It was probably me playing with my tits after I'd gone down on her.' She felt his cock surge against the inside of her thigh, and she shifted her leg to stroke against him. 'Are you trying to get details out of me, Daniel Alexander? Would you like to know how two women give each other multiples?'

He surged again, and she rolled over on top of him, guiding him into her wet cunt with one hand and settling on top of him, effectively pinning him beneath her. 'Maybe I should invite her over to join us. Not only could you see for yourself but you could have twice the pussy to smell. Would you like that?'

'Might do.' He held her gaze for a long moment. 'I'd be lying if I said I wouldn't love to see you two beautiful women going at it.'

She giggled. 'And maybe letting you join in just a little bit, hmmm? Or maybe we wouldn't want you to join in. Maybe we would just make you watch and wank. Your punishment for being so oblivious. What do you think?'

And suddenly there it was, guilt. He hadn't expected it. And it completely broadsided him. He was cheating on Francie now. Jesus, he hadn't even thought about her since Bel and Ellen had got into the limo all gropey and smelling of wet pussy. But as sure as anything, he really was cheating on her. He hadn't actually enjoyed sex with his wife in a very long time, but this, what had just happened between them, was mind-blowing stuff, and he knew, even as he lay there buried to the hilt in his wife's tight wet cunt, that he'd never be able to tell Francie about this. Never. This wasn't doing his husbandly duty. This was hot and nasty, the stuff of good porn films. And even if he did try to tell Francie, he had a queasy feeling in his gut that if Simon found out, he'd end up with a hell of a lot more than a hard slap on the face.

Feeling suddenly confused and wrong-footed, he was about to feign tiredness when Bel whispered in his ear. 'If you'd like Ellen to join us, I might be able to arrange it.' She gave his cock a playful grip inside her pussy. 'After all, we do have an awfully big bed.'

He had every intention of being incensed and telling her not only 'No', but 'Hell, no'. Instead, he said yes, he'd like that very much indeed, and then he fucked his wife one more time, just to give the guilt a nice sharp edge.

Chapter Eleven

Lavinia Haskins was a socialite's socialite. She briskly ushered them in and served them tea and homemade shortbread. Then she left them to their own devices to wander around the space she had planned for the potager, while she scurried off to a meeting with the board of one of the many charities she volunteered for. Introductions and tea on the fine bone china didn't take more than what Simon had no doubt was the allotted twenty minutes.

'It's clay all right, and fairly heavy,' Francie called over her shoulder, squeezing a handful of damp earth between her fingers. 'If she's wanting the garden in this year with anything like a decent yield next year, then it'll have to be raised beds.'

'That's what I would think,' Simon said.

'There are some lovely things we could do with raised beds here,' she said. 'And the odd shape of the space could make for some really innovative designs.'

He watched her walk around the site talking to herself, examining the soil, pacing off distances, checking the aspect. All the while she sketched and took notes in a small notepad she'd taken from her pocket. She was in her element. And God, he wanted her. She was most exquisite surrounded by fresh earth and plants and compost and sounds of the outdoors. He could understand completely why Dan was so totally besotted with her. And the fact that Simon knew what it felt like to have sex with her, to feel her incredible responsiveness, to hold her in his arms, made him want her all the more.

That she was only with him because of Dan made Simon's insides clench. She deserved better than Dan. Surely she had to know he'd never leave Bel for a gardener. Bel's family were old money, titled old money. The two were suited to each other. And Francie – well, Francie was suited to him, if she'd only open her eyes and see it.

He mentally shook himself. He couldn't believe he'd allowed himself to get drawn into this situation, to let it matter one way or another. He was having fabulous sex, something that running his own business gave him very little time for. Did it really matter what the arrangement was? Actually, when he thought about it, the

111

arrangement was ideal for a man in his position. He got hot, kinky sex at least once a week with no commitments. Just sex. Just satisfaction. Hadn't he actually fantasised about just that very thing after he broke up with Claire four years ago?

'I want to see your work.'

Her voice startled him out of his reverie. 'What?'

She waved a hand around the property. 'This doesn't seem like the place where one would want to build something that didn't blend in. I can assume if you've built Mrs Haskins a mediaeval maze, then perhaps it's a mediaeval theme I'll be working with as well, which is appropriate, actually. But I'd like to see what you've done, what you've built for her, so our styles won't clash. So we can blend.' As though she caught the implications of what she'd just said, she blushed hard, shoved her hands in the oversized pockets of her dress and looked down at her feet. 'I mean I think that's a good idea. Don't you?'

'Yes. Yes, of course it's a good idea.' He led her deeper into the grounds past the rose garden he had designed and the reflection pool he had restored. She gasped at the sight of the maze laid out before her, below the rise they stood on.

'Wow! It's …'

'Big.' He blushed. 'Yeah, I know. But that's the way she wanted it.'

She turned to meet his gaze. 'I was going to say it's wonderful.'

His first response was to kiss her for that, but she didn't give him time. She grabbed his hand and tugged him down the hill. 'Can you walk me through it or will we get lost?'

'Of course I can walk you through it. I designed it, didn't I?' Though he had to admit that being lost in the maze with her wasn't exactly a thought he couldn't live with. As they stepped into the tall dark alleyways of expertly clipped European box, he even toyed with the idea of getting them lost deliberately. But her ooohs and aahs, her soft laughter, her lovely work-hardened hands resting almost reverently against the smooth surface of the hedging made him feel deliciously young and giddy, made him feel like the two of them had discovered a wonderful secret world.

They walked in silence for a long time. The only sound, other than the odd chitter of a blue tit or the call of a blackbird, was their own breathing, rhythmic and deep, almost in perfect unison.

When they could no longer see the exit, when they were in the quiet depth of the maze, she turned to him so suddenly that he ran into her, crushing up against the firm softness of her breasts, feeling the always urgent press of her nipples gouging at his T-shirt. Her breath was suddenly fast, her eyes bright. 'Simon, it's exquisite. You're amazing.' Then she giggled. 'No pun intended.'

'And I'm in amazing company,' he breathed. He took the opportunity. He lifted her chin and brushed a kiss across her parted lips, and there was no denying the acceleration of her breath nor the slight flick of her tongue. She lifted her arms around his neck and yielded, as he deepened and expanded the kiss until he had no doubt they could both feel its effect in far-removed places. 'I want you,' he whispered, running splayed hands up over her ribs and her breasts. 'I want you so damned bad, Francie.'

And it was as though his words had suddenly woken her from a dream. She pushed him away, stepped back and shook herself. 'Not without Dan,' she said. 'Not without Dan. We'll be with him in just a few hours. We'll wait till then.' Then she turned and walked on ahead of him, leaving him feeling dark and tight.

They did have a meeting scheduled with Dan. This time in the summer house beyond the rose garden. He had sent them both a text this morning with no more information than the time and place. The bastard was probably enjoying the hell out of all this cryptic, spy-games, sneaking-around bullshit. It was typical of the Dan he'd known at uni. Some things never changed. Jesus, couldn't Francie see through his rubbish? It was so obvious to Simon. He was in half a mind not to play, just to tell them both to fuck off, that he was tired of being used.

114

But he wouldn't, because he wasn't. At least he wasn't tired of being used by Francie, however Francie needed to use him, and even he had to admit that it was outrageously hot sinking into her soft, wet pussy while Dan watched, only getting to wank.

When they came out on the other side of the maze back into the sunlight, she was all business, as though the kiss hadn't even happened. He mentally kicked himself for trying to make more of it, for trying to take it beyond where she was ready to go. And as she got into her car and said her goodbye, as he watched her drive away, in spite of the abortive attempt to take her in the maze, he was already anticipating their tryst at the summer house.

* * *

Francie arrived at the summer house early. She wore her usual wraparound dress and a red lace thong. She wished she could have waited. She wished she could have shown up fashionably late, but she couldn't, not when Simon seemed to have a penchant for showing up early. She felt a rush of guilt at how much she enjoyed time alone with him. In her mind she had already kicked herself, over and over, for not letting him take her in the maze. No doubt she'd have plenty of quality time with her vibe while fantasising about what might have happened. But guilt had gotten the better of her. She still loved Dan, and it couldn't be easy for him giving her to another man, watching another man have her, all the while knowing he couldn't touch her.

She entered the summer house to find Simon already there, slouched on the wicker love seat, his shoes and socks kicked to one side, his long bare toes wriggling in the warm sunlight. She offered him a smile and a blush, standing at the door suddenly shy, suddenly wanting to run back to the safety of the greenhouse. But he patted the space next to him, and she moved cautiously forward and sat. For a long time he said nothing. Then he spoke softly. 'I'm sorry. I was out of line in the maze. I shouldn't have touched you.'

She shook her head. 'No. No, it was me. I shouldn't have –' she nodded awkwardly '– escalated things.'

There was more silence, then he turned slightly to face her. 'So tell me, how did it happen between you and Dan? I mean you two don't exactly seem like a match made in heaven.'

'No, we don't, do we?' She slipped out of her blue gardening clogs and wiggled her toes next to his. 'I came back one morning from thinning carrots, and there he was in my greenhouse, pacing like a mad bull.' She chuckled and smiled to herself as it all came back to her. 'I'd never even met him before. I didn't know who he was. I grabbed a spade. I was well on my way to chasing him out when he managed to convince me that he was lord of the manor.'

Simon chuckled at the idea of Francie chasing Dan around the greenhouse with a spade. 'And what was his excuse?' he asked.

'He said he was thinking. He said he always came up to the greenhouse to think before Bel hired me on. He'd just forgotten that it was no longer unoccupied. A man who thinks. I liked that. I offered him tea and he spent the morning with me.' She looked up at Simon. 'When he left, I was in love.'

'That simple?' Simon half growled.

She shrugged. 'Nothing is ever that simple. I would have never acted on it. I would have never thought we'd see each other again, and then ...'

'And then?' Simon shifted closer to her. She could feel his intense gaze, and she couldn't keep from blushing.

'And then he caught me masturbating.'

'Jesus,' Simon whispered.

She nodded. 'I don't know what came over me, right there in the greenhouse sitting on the stool. Oh, I wasn't blatant or anything. I had one hand under my dress and the other inside to cup my breast.' She almost demonstrated before she caught herself. 'I was thinking about him, and suddenly he was standing there at the door. "Is that for me?" he asked. And when I tried to stop, he asked me to continue. The next thing I knew he had his cock out, and we were masturbating together.' Her laugh came out thin and breathless. 'In the beginning it was the hottest thing ever.'

Simon smoothed her hair away from her face. 'But you wanted more.'

She nodded, avoiding his gaze.

He lifted her fingers to his lips very carefully, as though he were afraid he might frighten her. 'And now you have more, Francie.' The warm touch of his lips sent tremors down her belly to her pussy.

'Now I have more.' She nodded, making no effort to pull her hand away.

He kissed her again. 'And now that you have more, is it enough? Is it enough like this?'

She didn't answer.

Chapter Twelve

'Darling, do hurry up in there. I have a surprise for you.' Bel's voice came from outside the bathroom door.

Shit, just what he didn't need right now, he was already running late to meet Francie and Simon. Only half dry from the shower, he shoved his way into his terry robe and pushed the bathroom door open in a cloud of steam. 'What is it, sweetheart? I'm going to be late and I really do need to ...' His words died in his throat. There, leaning back on a stack of pillows in the middle of the big four-poster bed sat Bel, completely naked except for a pair of lacy French-cut knickers. She wasn't alone. In a black satin thong and a matching bustier that barely contained her high, firm breasts reclined Ellen. She nursed hungrily at Bel's engorged nipples, while her hand rubbed and stroked its way down Bel's tight abdominal muscles ever closer and closer to the lacy knickers.

They both smiled up at him. 'Do come join us, darling,' Bel cooed. 'I have such a lovely gift for you.' She tugged lightly at the ribbon that held Ellen's breasts in check, and it gave just enough to reveal more of the lovely rise and fall of exquisite cleavage.

Dan's cock, which was already overheated with thoughts of Francie and Simon, was suddenly in danger of meltdown.

Bel grabbed him by the sash of his robe and tugged it open as she pulled him to the bed. 'Come on, darling, I can see by your big cock how uncomfortable you are. Ellen and I can take care of that for you.' She pushed aside his robe and Ellen gave a little-girl sigh of delight. 'We can make you feel so much better. It'll be so much fun, sweetheart. Do come and join us.' And she began to stroke his cock, using it like a lead until he was on the bed, and Ellen guided his hand to the lace at her bustier.

'Just one second,' he gasped. 'Let me cancel my appointment.' With fumbling fingers he pulled up the text he'd sent earlier to Francie and Simon and added:

Must cancel. Have an emergency meeting. Will make it up to you.

He sent it, tossed the phone on the bedside table and watched for a few minutes while the women fondled each other and kissed. Then Ellen turned her attention to him. She guided his cock into her mouth. Meanwhile Bel positioned herself behind the woman's lovely raised arse, pushed aside the crotch of her thong and began to give her pussy a proper tonguing. This was better than a wank. This was the best thing ever. And if Bel approved, Bel even instigated it, who was he to argue? And yet he had, for the second time, lied to Francie. There'd be hell to pay. The guilt flashed bright for a split second, then it was subsumed in the slippery sounds of two-deep oral sex, oral sex he was getting his fair share of from the infamous airy-fairy Ellen. And that was just the appetiser.

He curled his fingers in Ellen's hair and she purred like a kitten, then he reached down and made short work of the ribbon on the bustier, until anxious fingers could clasp heavy nipples, pinching and rolling until the kitten purr became a shivering moan that he felt all the way to the depth of his balls. Jesus, he had to be dreaming. This couldn't really be happening to him. But the thought dissipated rapidly into gasps and grunts of pleasure as Ellen went to working licking and sucking her way under his cock to his balls. Without losing her rhythm, she tugged and stroked his cock with her hand and gyrated and shifted back against Bel, who seemed to be doing her best to get as much of her face into Ellen's slick pout as possible, while her fingers danced over her own pussy.

As he watched her, he realised he'd never seen his wife masturbate before. He figured she did, but wow, how had he missed anything so hot? He could see from the in and out of her fingers how slick they were, how wet she was, how ready for a cock.

It took him a second to realise that, over the rounded hillocks of Ellen's arse, Bel's gaze was locked on him. Then she pulled away from Ellen's cunt, wiped her face on the back of her hand, and offered him a wicked smile. 'I could just keep playing with my little clitty until I come and my sweet juices dribble down my thighs on to the bed, unless ... Would you like to fuck my pussy for me, sweetheart?'

He nodded dumbly. There was a mad shuffling of naked bodies, and suddenly the women were in a delicious sixty-nine position with Bel's face once again in Ellen's cunt, but Ellen was now on her back and Bel's lovely lush quinny was right where Dan needed it to be. And he needed it really badly. When he ran his hand down to cup her juicy pussy, her little back hole clenched and quivered, and he couldn't resist. As he shoved his cock deep in her cunt, he began to finger her anus. She laughed a muffled laugh against Ellen's slit. 'If you want to fuck my little arsehole, darling, that's OK with me. Would you like that?' She stumbled over the last word as he slipped a second finger into her tight pucker and began to scissor the two. And she went wild, bucking and quivering all over with her first orgasm. Apparently her enthusiasm sent Ellen over the edge because the masseuse was suddenly jerking and convulsing underneath. Jesus, he couldn't even believe this was happening.

'There's lube,' Bel gasped when she could speak again. 'There's lube in the drawer, darling, to make it easier for you to put your cock in me. My little back hole is so tight and so sensitive, and do hurry. I need you there so badly.'

She didn't have to tell him twice. He found the lube and squirted probably way more than was necessary on to his cock, then rubbed the extra all over and around her quivering hole.

With her shoving back against him and him pushing his slippery cock into the tight yield of her sphincter, it all happened so fast. She was gasping and growling, and he was in deep and tight, weak in the knees, reminding himself that he'd never done this before, at least not to his wife, and wondering why the hell he hadn't.

And his wife was suddenly a wild woman he scarcely recognised. 'That's it, you fucking dirty bastard, hump my arsehole. You nasty son of a bitch, you didn't tell me you were such an arse fucker, but you are, aren't you? You want to squirt your load back there while Ellen eats my pussy, don't you? Don't you?' She reached around, grabbed him by the hair and literally snarled at him. 'You're such a filthy bastard.'

Christ, he'd never heard his wife talk like that before, and it made his balls feel like lead, it made him burn with an urgency that drove him to slam into her harder, his balls slap-slapping against her pussy with each thrust. Did she like this? Was this his Bel? He had no idea. But thinking was quickly becoming impossible as he reached the point of no return. As his load erupted full-force in the tight grip of her anus, she raged through her own orgasm while Ellen bucked against her.

Before he knew what was going on, almost before he could catch his breath, she pulled away, dismounted Ellen and turned on him. She bit him hard low on his belly just above his cock, and damn, it hurt! But fuck if he didn't like it! Then she stood, grabbed him by the cock and nodded towards the bathroom. 'Come on, darlings, I think we could all use a little shower.' Ellen followed close behind with her hand on his arse. If this was a dream, he sure as hell hoped he slept for a long time.

* * *

Dan was late. Very late. Francie sat slumped on the love seat next to Simon with her head resting on his shoulder. Through the open French doors they watched a song thrush hunting worms beneath the rose bushes. Simon found himself secretly thankful for every second Dan wasn't there. It was true, he couldn't have Francie until

Dan arrived, and then he could only have her as Dan wanted him to have her. Yet in so many ways he felt just being with her, sharing the garden, watching the birds, was having her a lot more than Dan would ever have her. He twisted a strand of her constantly mussed blonde hair around his finger.

She snuggled closer and sighed. 'Dan told me after our first time, after we masturbated together, why he would never be unfaithful to his wife.'

Simon raised an eyebrow in lieu of a response.

She continued. 'He said his father was constantly unfaithful to his mother, and she let it happen. Everyone knew. Everyone knew he'd slept with her maid of honour the night before the wedding.' She toyed with the tie that secured her dress. 'Apparently, when he was a little boy, Dan overheard his aunt talking with a friend about that little indiscretion.'

'His dad was still a randy bastard even when we were at uni together,' Simon said. He wondered why he'd never made that connection as to why Dan was so neurotic about being faithful to Bel. 'His mother was this sad little mousy thing. No one ever knew whether to feel sorry for her or feel contempt because she'd never stand up for herself. The whole situation was an embarrassment to Dan.'

'He told me,' Francie said. 'Anyway, he swore he'd never make his wife look like a fool the way his father had his mother. He vowed to be faithful until he could ask Bel for a divorce. And in a way that made it easier for me too. It eased my guilt because I wasn't really having sex with him, was I?' For a long moment she stared out into the garden lost in her own thoughts. 'But I would have. I would have even though I like Bel a lot.'

Simon bit his bottom lip and felt his insides knot. 'People don't think too clearly when their feelings are involved.'

'I've always thought clearly,' she said. 'I've always been the one who lets logic rule, the level-headed one. That was before this happened.' She glanced down at her watch, then stood and paced back and forth in front of the love seat. The sunlight rendered the skirt of her dress transparent, revealing the curve of her buttocks and the way the thong settled in between them against all the places he wanted to kiss and touch and make love to. It revealed the tiny V of lace covering her soft tight curls, nestling protectively above the part of her he wanted to open and spread and taste like sweet fruit.

He had just shifted to give his cock a little more space in the bind of his jeans when his cell phone beeped into the close summer air, and they both jumped.

He yanked it from his pocket, and she came to his side. 'Is it from Dan?' she asked.

He nodded. 'He's not coming.'

'What do you mean, he's not coming?' Francie grabbed the phone away from him and read:

Must cancel. Have an emergency meeting. Will make it up to you.

She handed the phone back to Simon and sat rigid on the edge of the love seat. He could see her pulse hammering in her neck. He could see the rise and fall of her throat as she swallowed hard. But there were no tears.

'I should go then,' he said softly.

She didn't reply, only sat there without looking at him.

'I can't make it tomorrow. I'm in Guildford all day.' He could smell her, like he could smell lavender in a garden at high summer long before he could see it. The smell of her sex he had memorised from the very first time he held her in his arms, but the rest of her scent had unfolded itself to him more slowly. The smell of outdoors was always on her, the smell of earth, the smell of clean female sweat. All of it, the whole of her, the rise and fall of her breasts as she breathed, the cadence of her breath, the heat radiating from her body, all of those things settled around him, tight-fitting and raw. 'I need to go,' he said again, resting a hand on the curve of her shoulder.

'No, you don't. You don't need to go.' She shrugged off his hand, popped up off the love seat and headed out the door of the summer house at a fast trot, leaving her garden shoes behind.

Still barefoot himself, he followed her across the warm grass out past the rose garden, over the hill into the mini wilderness that would become the Renaissance garden, and down to the deep pool at the edge of the stream. She undid the tie at the side of her dress and shrugged it off without breaking pace, stepped out of her thong and gave it a toss before she moved into the calm deep of the water, then dived under. For the tiniest fraction of a second, he feared she might mean herself harm. But she surfaced before he could even get his T-shirt off. She floated with her head back and the tips of her nipples breaking the surface. 'Well?' she called out. 'Are you coming or not? You can swim, can't you?'

'Of course I can swim.' He stripped off and stepped into the bright glare of the water. He was already erect, and her watching him did nothing to ease the pressure. 'You know what'll happen if I catch you?' he said, nodding down to his cock.

She swam towards him in an easy crawl stroke. 'You're assuming you'll have to catch me,' she said, and then she dove. It wasn't until he felt a tug on his hips and her mouth tightening around his cock that he figured out what she was up to.

'Jesus,' he gasped as she cupped and gently squeezed his balls. His feet were just barely touching ground. She seemed to be slowly pulling him with the nips and tugs of her mouth deeper and deeper until he had to tread water to keep his head from going under, careful not to kick her as he did so. And still she didn't surface.

'Francie,' he grunted. 'Francie, don't stay down too long.' But fuck, it felt so good, it felt so dangerously out of control as she sucked his cock then cupped his buttocks, then fingered his anus. Damn it! He wanted to bear down, he wanted to thrust, but the water held him in precarious weightlessness, and still she sucked and fondled. 'Oh God, Francie! Good Christ, Francie, please.'

One finger was buried knuckle-deep in his arsehole while the other hand kneaded his balls right on the border between pain and pleasure. And her mouth! Fuck, her mouth had him gripped and sucked in a tight wet paradise with her tongue flicking over the underside of his cock, and still she didn't surface.

'Francie … Francie, enough!' He grabbed her under the armpits and hauled her up. She surfaced enough to take a deep drag of air then she took his mouth, pulling him under in the process. And she held him there, her mouth on his, tongue darting, teeth nipping, gulping at him, and he gulped back even as his lungs cried out for oxygen. And just when he thought he'd have to manhandle her into shallow waters, she gave a powerful kick, moved into position, wrapped her legs around him, and his cock slipped into her tight grip just as his feet touched solid ground and the water broke over their heads. Oxygen raced back into starving lungs, taken in through their noses as they continued to eat and lap and nip at each other's mouths. He took her face in his hands and pulled her away enough that he could look into her eyes. 'Jesus, Francie, you scared me. I thought we were drowning.'

'We are, Simon,' she said, biting his lower lip then tightening her grip around his waist and matching his thrust. 'We are drowning.' He could tell by the tremors that began around his cock and shivered up her spine that she was coming. Her grip was far too tight and demanding for him not to follow suit.

They crawled to the grass at the edge of the stream, collapsed into each other's arms and fell asleep. When he woke up, the sun was setting and she was gone. He went to her cottage and knocked, but her car was gone and the place was dark and silent. There was nothing to do but go home and hope that he hadn't ruined everything. But then it was hardly his fault, was it? He really did try to practise some restraint. Somehow that didn't make him feel any better.

Chapter Thirteen

The sun was just setting when Simon unlocked the door to find Francie perched on the edge of an enormous brass bed that looked like it might have come from a brothel in a Western movie. The flood of relief at actually seeing her there, at knowing he hadn't lost her for ever, was tempered by all the questions threatening to burst his chest. She looked up at him, nodded her greeting and looked back out of the window.

'Nice place Dan picked out for us,' he said.

'Yeah. Nice.'

'Have you two … met here before?' he asked.

'No. We've never met off the estate. He would have considered this place too private. And he might have lost control.'

'Oh.'

There was a gaping moment of silence, then he mustered his courage. 'You left without saying goodbye.' He sat down cautiously next to her.

'I didn't know what to say,' she said softly.

He shrugged, trying to appear casual. 'So long, see you later, adios, gotta run. I don't know. Any of those would have probably done the trick.'

* * *

'I see you two had no trouble finding the place.' Dan burst into the charged atmosphere smiling ear to ear, bracing himself for the shit storm he expected for not showing up at the summer house. But, damn, it had been worth it. He never would have imagined his wife could be so fucking kinky.

Francie offered him a weak smile. 'Things happen.'

'Yes, they do.' The sudden wave of guilt was over-shadowed by relief. How many times had he had to contend with her temper when he was late or when he'd had to cancel, or even when he'd admitted to being with Bel? Wow, he wished he'd thought to bring Simon into the equation a long time ago. 'Well then, since you're both already sitting on the bed –' he nodded to Simon '– kiss her, and make her comfortable. That bed isn't just there for looks, you know?'

He pulled up a nearby chair and undid his fly. Bel was with her sister overnight and he, well, he had serious needs at the moment. The feel of his cock expanding into his hand made him suck his teeth. He watched as Simon's kisses became more demanding, and his hands cupped and caressed, still all on top of Francie's clothing, still all nice and proper. But his caresses were heading in the direction they were all anticipating. His hand brushed her breast, then moved to rest low on her belly as he eased her back on to the pillows.

Dan lifted his arse enough to slide his trousers and boxers down over his thighs. He felt the cool caress of the silk cushion against his buttocks as he settled himself into a comfortable spectator's position. 'Can you smell her sweet pussy, Simon?' he asked.

Simon nodded.

'Good, then take off her knickers. Oh, lovely,' he breathed, giving his balls a good cupping. 'A nice stretchy thong. Just perfect for what I have planned.'

Simon shot him a quick glance.

'Now I want you to take her wrists, both of them, over her head and tie them together to the headboard. With her panties.'

'What?' both Simon and Francie said at the same time.

He ignored Simon and spoke to Francie. 'Darling, we may be playing a little rougher today, but I wouldn't even consider leading us in this direction if I didn't

133

think you'd enjoy it. Are you OK with that?'

Her face was still flushed with the first bloom of arousal, but he was pretty sure there was the tiniest twinge of fear mixed in now, thanks to his request. Her nipples pressed tight and high against the dress. His balls felt lead-heavy at the sight of her, still fully clothed except for the smallest glimpse of her fragrant cunt peeking from under the hem of her scrunched skirt. 'Sweetheart?'

She held his gaze for another moment, then released a slow controlled breath and nodded to Simon, who knelt on the bed next to her with her knickers in his hand.

There was no missing the way she ground her bottom into the thick down of the duvet as he stretched over her, nearly covering her with his body in his efforts to bind her hands. A nice move, Dan thought. 'Make sure she's good and secure, Simon. We don't want her thrashing about and getting loose on us, do we?' Once again there was the flash of fear in her eyes, and the look Simon shot him was not nice at all.

'Now, darling, Simon and I are going to play a little game with you. And for your part, two things will be essential. You will keep your eyes shut at all times and you'll not speak unless you're told to. Is that clear?'

She nodded, looking so much like a frightened rabbit that he nearly decided to forget the whole idea.

'Simon?'

Simon offered only the slightest of nods.

'Perfect. Now then, just one more thing, darling. If you do forget those simple rules, if you speak or open your eyes, you'll be punished.' Slowly, carefully, so that he was certain they both understood his intentions, he slid the belt from his trousers one loop at a time.

Francie's eyes were wide, pupils dilated, but she said nothing.

Simon cursed out loud. 'Francie, you don't have to do this. We don't have to do this.'

Holding Dan's gaze, she nodded slowly. 'It's all right, Simon. I'm all right with this.' She looked up at him. 'If you are.'

Again there was the slightest hint of a nod.

'Good, then close your eyes, Francie darling, and no peeking. I'll know if you do.' Dan slapped the looped belt against his hand. 'And not a word, not a peep until we've all had a good come. Are we clear?'

She nodded, and her eyes fluttered shut.

'That's my girl. Now, Simon, there's a nice Victorinox knife in the drawer of the bedside table. Oh, don't look at me like that! It's only to remove Francie's dress. Silly me, I forgot to have you take it off before we tied her, and now I'm afraid the only way we can get her completely naked is to cut it off. Go on then. Do the honours. That's right, slit it. Right down the front, right down between her lovely tits so we can see them and play with them. All the way. All the way down. We want nothing keeping your cock from her lovely cunt.'

Simon was extra careful, as Dan knew he would be, and Francie's body was tight with that delicious frisson of fear. Her breasts and belly were sheened in a soft glow of perspiration. She sucked a harsh breath as Simon slit the dress under the arms and shoved it away. And oh, yes, Simon was rock hard.

And he wasn't the only one. Dan's cock felt like concrete as he watched the action on the bed. 'Take off your jeans, Simon. That's it; give your cock some breathing room. Now let Francie taste you. Is that pre-come I see already? You like having her tied up a lot more than you're letting on, don't you? Your body doesn't lie, Simon, your body doesn't lie.'

Simon growled something incoherent and positioned himself so that Francie had little choice but to take his cock in her mouth. Her eyelids fluttered rapidly, and she moaned softly, but she took him. She even pushed forward on to him until she nearly gagged herself, until he curled his fingers in her hair to regulate her movement. But Dan could tell he wanted to thrust with abandon. The muscles of his buttocks tightened and strained with each thrust, and the clench of his arsehole reminded Dan of what he had done to Bel's lovely anus, when they shared their bed with Ellen. It reminded him of what the two women had done to his in turn when they had dragged him off to the shower. It was their delicious rough play that had inspired his plan for Francie and Simon.

'That's enough,' he grunted. 'Simon, I can see by the way Francie's little arse is grinding and thrusting that her pussy needs some attention. Feel her for me. Is she wet?'

Simon slid down until he lay next to Francie on his side and ran his hand over her belly, careful so that she always knew where he was. For a tiny second he cupped her pubis, then he slipped two fingers over her heavy clit and down between her distended lips. The catch of his breath, the quiver that went all the way up Francie's spine and ended in a sharp gasp at the back of her throat told Dan all he needed to know.

'She needs to come badly, doesn't she, Simon?'

'Yes. Yes, she does,' Simon replied. And it wasn't hard to tell that it was his intention to make her come.

'Leave her,' Dan said, pressing a thumb to the underside of his cock to keep from losing control way before the scenario he had fantasised played itself out. With the other hand he motioned to Simon to come to his side. Francie squirmed and whimpered slightly as he took his hand away from her pussy, and in sheer defiance he dropped a kiss on to her mound. That's all right, Dan thought. Let him be defiant. It would make everything else better. As Simon came to stand by his side, his cock leading the way, Dan raised a finger to his lips, and they both turned their attention to Francie, sprawled spread-eagled on the bed, nipples erect, pussy swollen and distended with desire. They watched silently, holding their breath, and their cocks, as Francie began to squirm against herself. When Simon would have gone to her, Dan grabbed his wrist and raised the warning finger to his lips once more.

They watched in thick, heavy silence, the air around them smelling of sex not quite satisfied. Francie stopped squirming. The pulse in her throat jumped. She held her breath, cocked her head, and listened. And still Dan held Simon in check.

The heavy stretching of time did nothing to ease the load in either man's balls, nor to make their heavy erections any less hard. Whether Francie was listening intently or trying in vain to get some relief, watching her, just watching her, was a source of deep, ball-wrenching arousal.

And then it happened: her eyelids fluttered once, then again. She opened one eye, just a slit, then shut it quickly, but not quickly enough.

Dan tut-tutted. 'Francie, Francie, I always knew you were a wild, undisciplined thing at heart, and here you are disobeying my simplest order. I didn't ask you to do anything very difficult, did I?'

She shook her head.

'Come, Simon. We'll have to punish her now.' He ran the belt through his hand.

Simon shook his head hard. 'No fucking way. I'm not going to use that on her.'

'Francie, darling, Simon is squeamish. Are you? If you are we can end this now, and all go home unsatisfied to wank alone. That's all right, darling. I'm sure we've all three had our share of solitary masturbation.'

Simon growled something derogatory under his breath, but Dan noticed his cock was no less erect.

'Will you take your punishment, darling, or shall we call it quits? Oh, don't worry, sweetheart, I have a nice new dress hanging in the closet for you. I won't send you home naked. Now what will it be? Will you take your punishment?'

The room was electric with anticipation. Simon positively bristled. Francie's eyelids flickered hard but she kept them closed, then she offered a nod. If Dan could read anything into it, he figured it was probably delicious defiance, and that thought made his cock surge even tighter. 'That's my sweet girl. That's my lovely Francie.'

Simon stepped away and shook his head. 'No. I won't do it. I won't hit her.'

Dan ran the belt through his fingers. 'It's a spanking, Simon, it's not the same. It's completely consensual, and I'm not asking you to do it. I'm going to do it.'

'What?' both Simon and Francie gasped at the same time.

'I won't be touching her.' He ran the looped edge of

the belt up the inside of her thigh, and she gasped and quivered. 'Only the belt will be touching her and, Francie dear, it will be touching you a little less gently, since you just broke the rules again by speaking.' There was a gasp but nothing more. Then he turned his attention to Simon. 'You're going to hold her for me, hold her so I have access to her lovely little bottom. Francie, if you're all right with this would you please reassure Simon, who still seems to be a little uncertain, though his cock definitely isn't.'

Francie nodded hard, and Simon moved to her side, resting his hand on her thigh so she'd know where he was.

'Now, I need to shed the rest of these clothes.' Dan began to strip. 'Simon is already quite naked, darling, as you'll soon find out, and I need to be too, since I intend to get quite sweaty from your punishment.'

'Jesus,' Simon whispered, moving protectively closer to Francie.

Once Dan was stripped, he came to the side of the bed opposite Simon. 'Now, lift her legs for me, Simon. That's right, on to your shoulder, that's good, now I have perfect access to her naughty little bottom.' The words were barely out of his mouth before he brought the flat of the belt down with a smack against her arse cheek. She gasped, but said nothing. Simon, however, swore aloud, and there was no doubt at whom his curses were directed.

'She behaves better than you do, Simon,' Dan said as he brought the belt down again with a sharp thwack. 'Feel her,' he ordered. 'Feel her pussy.'

Simon slid his hand gently in between her thighs and gasped.

'She's wet, isn't she? Isn't she?' He didn't need to hear the answer. He could see that Francie was doing her best to hump Simon's hand. 'That's enough. Naughty girls have to take their punishment before they get their pouting little pussies fucked, don't they?' He gave her another smack with the belt. 'Don't they, Francie?'

Francie nodded and squeezed her eyes shut tighter. Her chest rose and fell like bellows, her nipples were swollen and heavy and deep cherry red. And God, he nearly came just looking at her all trussed up and distressed and horny as hell.

'This is not funny,' Simon growled.

'Of course it's not funny. It's not meant to be funny. But it's working on a lot of other levels.' Dan nodded towards Simon's erection, which looked almost as ready to burst as his did.

The next three smacks came in quick succession with Francie bucking and straining so hard that it was a struggle for Simon to hold her. In spite of his best efforts to stay focused, Dan's hand, the one not wielding the belt, pulled at his cock in hard, tight strokes.

He trailed the belt down between her arse cheeks and

along her tightly clenched thighs, certain he couldn't hold out much longer. 'Have you learned your lesson yet, darling?' he asked.

She nodded desperately, her hips thrusting and grinding in spite of Simon's firm hold on her.

'Put her down then, Simon.'

As Simon lowered her bottom on to the bed she winced and sucked air, but she said nothing. Simon did that for her, but Dan ignored him.

'You're such a naughty girl, Francie. You've made my cock so hard while I punished you. And Simon's too. Goodness, I think we're both about to burst, and you there with your arse in the air and your pussy so wet and juicy that the whole room smells of you. You've made us all so terribly uncomfortable, being such a slut. And now I think you need to let Simon fuck you, give the poor man some relief. And I'll watch the two of you rut while I have a good hard wank. What do you think, Simon? No, don't untie her, and Francie, not a word from you. Keep your eyes shut. And you don't come until Simon and I have come. Are you clear?'

Her eyes were clenched tight and she was breathing fire, he could tell, but she nodded. 'Good girl.' He turned his attention to Simon. 'You can fuck her now.'

Simon wasted no time. He climbed on to the bed. Her legs were already spread, and she arched her back and moaned her need, wincing as he positioned himself and yet still thrusting her pussy towards him until she was completely impaled. Then she wrapped her legs around him and shoved and grunted. He pushed up into her and lifted her so that her tender bottom was off the bed, then he grabbed the headboard on either side of her hands for leverage and began to thrust hard.

Dan sat on the edge of the bed as close as he could get without touching her, tugging and yanking on his cock until his arm ached, so hot, so desperate, so unable to believe he had actually done what he just did.

The headboard slammed noisily into the wall with Francie and Simon's combined efforts. Francie's breasts bounced and swayed and her head thrashed from side to side, occasionally banging against the headboard. Simon came first, roaring his release, pulling Francie to him until she was practically doubled in half beneath him. Then he ripped at her ruined knickers to free her wrists, and as her arms shot around his neck, it was more than Dan could take. He came hard, shooting his wad across the expensive duvet just missing Simon's bare arse. And Francie, true to her word, came last. She came in hard, silent shudders, in deep-chested moans that never left her throat. Her arms were wrapped around Simon's neck, her hands in white-knuckled fists against the top of his back. But her eyes were clenched tightly shut. It was then Dan noticed that Simon was whispering her name over and over into her ear. At last, with Simon holding her to him in a spoon position and Dan facing her, his fingers curled lightly in her hair, they all fell asleep.

* * *

It was long towards morning when Francie woke to the sound of a tawny owl in the oak tree outside the window. Dan now lay with his back to her, breathing the deep, even breath of sleep. But Simon, Simon was even closer to her if that were possible. His hand had migrated down to curl protectively against her mons, and as she shifted, ever so slightly, his middle finger eased forward to stroke the swell of her clit. His erection pressed low against the crack of her arse. Her bottom still ached from the spanking, but she ignored it. It was almost unconscious: the shifting, the slight opening, the definite acceleration of breathing and pulse rate. But his finger was most definitely stroke-stroke-stroking her clit, then dipping slightly down into the sticky wet warmth between her labia and spreading it like honey over some luscious sweet.

She opened her legs, only the tiniest bit, and he took advantage, scissoring two fingers up inside her and thumbing her clit. She could feel the rocking of his hips keeping the insistent press of his cock tight against the juncture of her thighs. His face nuzzled her neck and she felt his lips part, his tongue stroke and flick, his teeth rake. All the while his breath raised the fine hair up her spine, feeling like it dispersed little bits of his essence all over her body, delicate shimmering bits that caressed even the places she had never been able to touch. The moon was full, bathing the room in monochromatic shimmers, and it was as though she were in another world, a world peopled only by Simon and her. Carefully, quietly, she pulled her leg forward until she felt her pussy gape for him. His hand abandoned her clit and slid over her hip and down low between her buttocks to finger her open. She held her breath, the pounding of her heart in her ears so loud she feared it would surely wake Dan. Then she lifted her leg, just enough, and he pressed forward, scooching and wriggling almost as a sleeper might in his secret encounters in the dream world. But it wasn't sleep or dreams that moved him, and, with a thrust that was sharp yet still somehow stealthy, he pushed into her and with a quiet shudder they released the collective breath they had been holding.

The shifting was almost unnoticeable. Other than his fingers strumming her clit, everything was happening up inside her pussy. Every grasp, every clench felt like a small earthquake; every raking of flesh against flesh felt like flint against steel, igniting a quiet inferno. Every single movement became tighter, smaller, more focused, more exquisite. She felt his nipples pressing into her back, she felt the slight scratch of the stubble on his jaw that hadn't been there a few hours ago, she felt the tight in-and-out of his diaphragm as his body fought for oxygen, and it all culminated in an orgasm that reverberated up through her and back down to meet his own shuddering ejaculation.

As their breathing steadied and stilled, Simon pressed a lingering kiss to her ear and whispered so softly that she wondered later if she had imagined it. 'He's married, Francie. But I'm not.'

Chapter Fourteen

'My cock's hard, darling,' Dan said.

'I'm terribly sorry about that, sweetheart,' Bel replied.

He leaned against the bedpost shifting uncomfortably in his jeans while he watched his wife. She stood in front of the full-length mirror in a pale-blue bra with a matching thong and a pair of impossibly high, impossibly colour-coordinated stilettos. In each hand she had a sexy, stylish sundress that she held up to her chest in turn.

'Which one do you think looks best, Daniel?'

'The one with the little flowery things,' he said absently while he undid his fly.

'They're not flowers. They're little tiny paisleys,' she said, hanging the other dress back on the closet door and holding the one Dan had chosen up in front of her, studying her reflection.

'Right, paisleys. Bel, sweetheart, I need to come, and you flashing your lovely tight bottom at me isn't making me need it any less.'

She rolled her eyes and tossed her hair. 'I'm not flashing my bottom at you darling, I'm trying to get ready for an appointment. You're just ogling me. That's all.'

He lifted his cock free and began to stroke, knowing she could see his reflection in the mirror, knowing she'd like that. 'Are you going to see Ellen?'

'Yes, dear, I'm going to see Ellen.'

'She'll like that dress, and the thong,' he said.

'Yes, she will, Daniel. Blue's her favourite colour.'

'And will you let her lick your pussy?'

'Possibly. She's very good at that sort of thing, you know.'

'Yes, I know.' He shoved out of his trousers and came to stand behind her rubbing his hard-on against the crack of her arse. 'But she can't give you this.'

She giggled. 'Honestly, you men think your cocks are God's gift to the universe.' She tried to elbow him away but not very hard.

'So what's your point?' he said with a hip thrust that unbalanced her enough for him to snake a hand in and unhook her bra, pushing it aside to cup her breasts.

'Dan! I'll be late.'

He slipped one hand down over the tight flatness of her belly and into the front of her thong to give her clit a stroke, then he tongued her earlobe. 'Cancel.' He bit gently and tugged; his fingers dipped into the tell-tale moistness of her cunt. 'Tell her your husband needs to come, and you have to fuck him. Tell her your wifely duties come first.' He tweaked her clit hard, and she jumped, making her lovely full breasts bounce and jiggle lusciously, and he could see every detail reflected back in the mirror.

She wriggled and raked back against him. 'But what about Ellen's poor little pussy? Who'll make her come if I cancel?'

'I'm sure she'll manage just this once. She's got fingers, hasn't she?' He gave a demonstrative swish up inside her cunt, then he pushed his cock in between the top of her thighs and dry humped.

She offered him her best exasperated sigh. 'All right then, hand me my phone.'

He did as she asked, and she punched in the number, feigning irritation. 'This is the second time in two weeks, Daniel. Ellen won't be pleased.'

He pulled the crotch of her thong aside and tugged and stroked her burgeoning labia, causing her to shift daintily from foot to foot, bowing her legs slightly. 'Tell her she can come over and punish me. You can both punish me together.'

As Bel made the call, he dropped to his knees behind her and tongued her anus, feeling the flood of her response against his fingers now scissoring in her cunt.

When she finished the call, he took the phone from her and tossed it on the bed, yanked aside the thong and pushed into her from behind. He wasn't wrong, she was wet and grasping and ready for him. Her clit felt like a hard little marble under the press and stroke of his thumb. He wasn't gentle. She didn't like gentle. Imagine it taking him all this time to discover that about her. With each thrust her heavy breasts, now free of the bra, bounced forward towards the mirror. It was an exquisite view, close-ups of her breasts, close-ups of the scrunch and strain of pleasure on her beautiful face.

The sight of her made the load he was carrying feel all the weightier, made his need for a good emptying all the more urgent, which was amazing considering he'd come only a few hours ago. He slammed into her hard, forcing her perfectly made-up cheek and the heavy sway of her breasts against the mirror just as she began to wail, 'Oh God, Dan, I'm coming! I'm coming!' And he wasn't far behind.

Afterwards, as they snuggled down on the bed together, half dozing, she breathed a happy sigh and stroked his damp cock, which now rested at half-mast against his thigh. 'Ellen's going to punish you so hard.'

He chuckled softly. 'Well, I do deserve it, don't I?'

He deserved it all right. More than she knew. But, Jesus, he had the best of all worlds right now. He had never imagined his wife could be so slutty and so adventurous. These days he couldn't get enough of her. And Ellen was just icing on the cake. Then there was Francie. She now seemed perfectly happy for him to watch and wank, now that Simon was in the picture. Dan always knew he was a bit of a voyeur, but he'd never dreamed he'd be watching something as filthy as the two of them, and they were almost at his beck and call. And best of all, there had been no mention of the divorce for some time now. To be honest, he certainly didn't want to rock the boat when Bel seemed to be doing so well.

He'd already been with Francie and Simon early in the day. He had watched Simon make Francie stuff her hot little cunt with a dibber or some such. He'd never heard of it before, but it looked a bit like a dildo on one end, sharpened to a dull point at the other. Jesus, gardening could be so erotic! Anyway, Simon had her sopping before he mounted her and rode her on the staging table in the greenhouse. Dan had shot his wad all over Francie's bare tits, and Simon, he thought Simon would never stop coming.

Oh, there was still guilt, but it was amazing to him how much easier guilt was to manage when everyone seemed to be filthy, nasty and willing to fuck.

* * *

Thankfully it was one of those days when Francie had a million little maintenance tasks to do in the beds and in the greenhouse, and Simon was equally swamped. If there had been time, she doubted very seriously if she could have resisted another go with him after Dan left. When she had fucked Simon in the stream, she had been angry with Dan for not showing up. That was her excuse. Afterwards when the guilt raged, she'd promised herself she'd not let it happen again. But the next time they made love, it had been right there in the same bed with Dan. And what she felt in the dark of night when there was no place she could run to, nothing she could do to take her mind off things, what blossomed in her chest for Simon was a complication she didn't need.

Nothing out of order had happened since; only the sex that Dan planned and the three of them shared. But she feared that was just because the last couple of times they'd been together, either she or Simon had had other commitments they couldn't get out of, and there had been no time to linger beyond what Dan required of them.

Jesus, had it come to that? What Dan required of them? She loved Dan. Didn't she? Then why did she think about Simon all the time? She thought about the way his hands worked the soil. She thought about the way his feet set so firmly on the ground when they walked in the garden together, like he was connected, like he had roots that went deeper than the trees in Dan's arboretum. She thought about the way he felt when she touched him, the way he smelled, the way his eyes lit up when he shared his plans for Dan's Renaissance garden. She thought about Simon all the time, Dan not so much, and that stoked the guilt constantly. Bel certainly seemed to be doing well these days. Francie figured it would only be a matter of time till Dan would ask her for the divorce. And then what? The idea of Simon no longer being in her life was unthinkable. The thought of betraying Bel not much less so. It would all get so messy. And then Bel would hate her. And Simon would be gone.

She was so lost in her thoughts that it took her a while to realise she was no longer alone. She looked up from thinning cauliflower seedlings in the nursery bed to find five expensively dressed women, plus Mrs Lavinia Haskins and Bel, looking down at her.

'Francie, darling.' Bel stepped forward. 'Lavinia has been showing me the sketches you've made for her … what's it?

'Potager,' Mrs Haskins supplied.

'That's right, potager,' Bel continued. 'You've been holding out on me, haven't you, darling?'

Francie wiped her hands on her dress tail and stood. 'I didn't think it mattered. I mean I do it all on my own time.'

Bel waved a hand as though she were about to conduct an orchestra. 'Of course you do, darling, of course you do. I know that. I think it's great for you to have a creative outlet. And apparently you're so creative that Lavinia told her friends and, well, we all share the same massage therapist, so it wasn't long before word got around, and you're the talk of the town. Then everyone found out you work for me, and of course they just had to come see your creative genius at work.'

Lavinia Haskins nodded. 'We all want a piece of you, darling. We had no idea Bel was being so naughty, keeping someone so delicious all to herself.'

Francie felt a clench of excitement in her chest that they were here to see her, to see her garden, and they couldn't have come at a better time. It was high summer and the raised beds were now at their best. Everything was lush and green and laden with either fruit or buds. 'This is not a potager,' Francie said. 'This is a fully functional walled kitchen garden, and it has been for probably as long as the house has been here.' She nodded towards the ageing brick wall that surrounded the beds.

'Lovely, isn't it?' Bel added proudly, 'It was a real shambles until Francie took things in hand.'

'I want one of these,' one of the women spoke up. 'I've already got a wall back behind the house in Somerset. It's all grown up now. You reckon it could have been a mediaeval kitchen garden at one time?'

154

'I'm sure Francie can tell you if she sees it, Elizabeth,' Bel said. Then she offered Francie a bright smile. 'Darling, could you be an angel and show us around? I'll have Cook make tea.' Bel pulled her mobile from her pocket to make arrangements for refreshments. And for the next thirty minutes Francie felt like the guest presenter of *Gardeners' World*, fielding questions on propagation techniques, giving a crash course in essential kitchen garden tools and showing off her brassicas and sweetcorn. Of course everyone was interested in her basil plants.

She potted up a young basil for each of them and made appointments in her diary to come and check out their properties and discuss what they wanted. Then they all trotted off to the conservatory for tea, an event she was able to wriggle out of, being covered in compost and sweat and having lots more thinning and pruning to do before she could get the late French beans sown.

She knew Simon was working in the Renaissance garden today, and in spite of her best efforts to stay focused, she couldn't keep fantasies of accidentally running into him out of her head. In her mind's eye, they were already naked in the stream, and she had her legs wrapped around him.

'Hey, gorgeous, you wouldn't happen to be the veg lady, would you?'

She turned from the sink where she was washing out seed trays. The man standing in front of her wore a white polo shirt just tight enough to show off the shape of his sculpted pectoral muscles with their very erect nipples. The shirt was tucked neatly into chinos just tight enough to hint at a substantial package. His blond hair and tanned face were airbrush perfect, and when he smiled she needed sunglasses for protection from the dental glare.

'I'm the kitchen gardener, if that's what you mean. Is there something I can do for you?'

He leaned in so that his hip rested against the sink, a little too near her personal space, and offered her his minty-breathed blinding smile. 'I certainly hope so.'

She wiped her hands on the towel and stepped back. 'Look, I'm just the gardener. If you want to see Mr or Mrs Alexander, you'll have to go to the house, or I can call them for you on my mobile if you'd like.' She reached in her pocket.

But he shook his head and was suddenly serious. 'No! No I don't want to see them. It's definitely you I came to see, Franny.'

'It's Francie,' she said, taking another step back. 'My name is Francie, and what do you want?' She tried to keep the irritation out of her voice.

'Francie, oh, right. Sorry. Well, Francie –' the big smile was back '– I'm dying to know all about kitchen gardening. I mean I can understand in a small flat that you might try to plant a few things on your kitchen windowsill, a few herbs, maybe a cherry tomato, that sort of thing. But in a place like this, and with that big plot out there, I wouldn't think planting anything in the kitchen would be necessary.'

She folded her arms across her chest and swallowed back as much of her impatience as she could manage. 'Look, why are you here? Clearly you aren't interested in gardening and I'm really busy.'

Suddenly the air outside the greenhouse was alive with the sound of women talking and oohing and aahing over brassicas and beans, and Bel burst in. 'I'm sorry, Francie, but everyone just had to have another look.' She stopped just inside the door and looked from Francie to Airbrush Man and back again. 'Francie, darling, who is this?'

'I have no idea,' Francie replied. 'He just showed up.'

'Well, hello.' He offered Bel his hand. 'I'm Darrell, and who might you be?'

'Don't be ridiculous, you're not Darrell. I know Darrell. He's the big tough-looking strappy bloke who's been spending a lot of time with our Francie lately.' She flashed Francie a knowing smile.

'What?' Both Airbrush Guy and Francie said at the same time.

'No, really, I am Darrell.'

Just then the women in the garden burst into the greenhouse in a wave of Chanel and designer smart-casual, and stopped almost in unison. 'Darrell?' Lavinia

Haskins said, running a hand through her hair. Several other women seemed to be doing a bit of preening too at the sight of the only male present. 'Darrell, darling.' She moved into the room and kissed him lightly on each cheek. 'Lovely to see you. What are you doing here?' And suddenly the man was engulfed in hugs and kisses all around while Bel and Francie stood staring.

'I think that's Darrell,' Francie said.

'Of course he's Darrell,' Lavinia said. 'And is he spending the evening with you, Francie darling? But I thought you were with Simon.'

'Who's Simon?' Bel asked. Lavinia couldn't exactly be accused of guffawing, but it was probably as close as someone of her station got. 'Oh, my dear Bel, you thought Simon, the landscaper, was Darrell. Did you hire Darrell as a little surprise for our Francie? What, is it her birthday? The anniversary of her working for you? Oh, do tell me. Mind you, I certainly think Simon would make a fabulous escort, if he ever decides to moonlight,' she added as an afterthought.

Darrell offered Lavinia a full-lipped pout. 'Does this mean I have competition, ladies?'

'Escort?' Francie suddenly felt like her cheeks would burst into flame. 'Why would you think I'd want an escort?'

The greenhouse fell into total silence, and all attention suddenly shifted from Francie to Bel and back again.

'Oh, darling, please don't be angry.' Bel squeezed Francie's hand, not seeming to notice it was wet and grubby. 'I hired Darrell to come see you. Mind you, nothing more than a chat, maybe dinner and drinks unless you wanted more, of course. I was so afraid we were going to lose you after Cook heard you talking to some bloke about another job, and I told Dan, and neither one of us could bear the thought of losing you.' She took a deep breath. 'And Dan told me he'd take care of it, and I should have believed him, because it turns out I didn't need to hire Darrell because he'd already hired Simon.'

'What?' Francie extricated her hand suddenly feeling light-headed.

'Ah ha,' Lavinia Haskins said. 'So Simon *is* working as an escort then. Well, I have no doubt he'll be very popular.'

Darrell pouted, and she patted his arm in reassurance.

Bel took Francie's hand again. 'And Francie darling, you seem so much happier since Dan introduced you to Simon, who I thought was Darrell.'

'I was away in the Canary Islands with a client,' Darrell supplied. 'I just got back yesterday.'

Everyone ignored him. All attention was now on Bel and Francie. Bel continued. 'We only ever wanted you to be happy. We thought if you were happy, and you were happy *here*, then you wouldn't take another job.

We didn't know you meant something creative on the side. Honestly, darling, we had no idea, and Cook can so easily get her facts mixed up, you know. But the dear thing means well, doesn't she?'

Just then Simon and Dan walked through the door, their casual clothes and muddy boots indicating they'd been down checking out the progress in the Renaissance garden. 'What's this, a party?' Dan said, offering a genial smile.

Francie swayed slightly. The whole room suddenly seemed too hot and too close. She dropped the towel and moved in slow motion to stand in front of the two men. 'That's Darrell,' she said. 'Bel hired him to entertain me.' She blinked hard to fight back the tears she absolutely would not let interfere with her anger.

Both men shot a glance at Darrell, then Bel. Dan's face went white, Simon's red.

Francie took a deep breath and continued. 'But poor Darrell's a bit late, isn't he?'

The greenhouse was dead silent. Even the women simpering over Darrell held their breath. 'You told me Simon was your best friend. You told me he was your gift to me. You told me he had agreed to do this for us, as your friend. You begged me to do this for you, or I never would have …' She shook her head. 'Francie, you don't understand. I didn't … I wouldn't …' Simon reached for her hand but she slapped him away.

160

'And you?' She looked up into his grey eyes, now blurring through her unshed tears. 'Well, I guess I'm not the only one who accepted a job on the side, am I?' She frantically wiped her eyes. 'I hope he paid you well.' Then, as though someone else inside her took control, she turned to her enthralled audience, cleared her throat and raised her chin. 'Ladies, Darrell, if you'll excuse me, I'm finished here.'

She grabbed her bag from under the staging table and made a run for it. She heard Simon shouting after her, she heard the eruption of chaos from inside the greenhouse, but she ignored it all and made straight for her car.

Chapter Fifteen

Bel paced the parquet floor of her study like an enraged bull. The two men shifted uncomfortably on the sofa. When Francie had driven away, spinning a rut in the lovely white pea gravel in front of her cottage, Bel had insisted, none too gently, that Simon join her and Dan in the house for a little chat. The other women had gladly taken Darrell off to a pub somewhere.

Bel's face was pale, and from her clenched fists it looked like she seriously wanted to hit someone. Simon imagined he was included on her list of candidates right along with Dan. She squared her shoulders and spoke without looking at them. 'You were both having sex with Francie then?'

'I was,' Simon said. 'He wasn't.'

Her cast-iron gaze settled on Dan. 'Then you were what, Daniel? Watching? Cheering them on? What?' Her voice broke in breathless disbelief.

Both men nodded.

She paced. 'You expect me to believe that after ...'

'After what my father did, that I didn't fuck her? Is that what you were going to say? Like father, like son?' Dan's voice was low, barely audible. He stared into space, avoiding her gaze.

Her chin quivered. 'I was going to say after you caught me with Ellen. I mean I could have understood. I would have wanted to ...' Her voice drifted off.

'I didn't say I didn't want to. I said I didn't do it. I watched and wanked. I never touched Francie, even before Simon came into the picture.'

'Then when you found out Francie might leave us, you hired Simon?'

Simon bristled.

Dan shook his head. 'I tried to blackmail him,' he said. 'And then I tried to hire him to have sex with Francie. In the end all I had to do was let nature take its course. They were already attracted to each other. It didn't take long before I knew it was more than attraction.' He heaved himself up off the sofa and stood next to Bel. 'By that time it didn't really matter. Things were better with you again, and I guess I figured if you felt comfortable enough bringing Ellen into our bed then you

163

wouldn't mind me watching Simon and Francie and having a wank.'

She turned on him so fast Simon thought she would slap him. 'Never mind poor Francie's feelings in all this. Did either of you ever consider that?' Simon started to speak but she pointed a very well-manicured nail at him. 'You shut up. I'm not talking to you.'

She looked up into Dan's eyes and held him as surely as if she'd tied him to a chair. 'Do you love me, Daniel?'

Dan released a harsh breath and even in the dim light Simon could see the man's eyes mist. 'Of course I love you, Bel, I always have. Always.'

She grabbed him by the hair and pulled him to her, pulled him into a kiss that had to be painful. And when she released him he would have lost his balance and toppled back on to the couch if she hadn't had a fist still curled in his hair. 'Then the next time your cock wants to wander, you take me with you. We do this together or no deal, do you understand?'

'I understand,' he breathed.

'And you.' She turned to Simon.

Simon found himself sitting at attention, shoulders squared, eyes straight ahead.

'Do you love Francie?'

The somersaulting and hammering of his insides made him think for a second that he might be having a heart attack, but he knew that wasn't the problem. 'Yes,' he said. It was the only thing he could say that mattered, and he knew it. 'Yes, I love her.'

'Then go find her and make it right.' She nodded towards the door. 'And don't be such a twat this time.'

'And you.' She snapped her fingers at Dan and pointed to the oak staircase. 'Upstairs. I'm not finished with you yet.'

As he turned to go, Simon just caught a glimpse of her slender suede belt clearing the first loop of her trousers. He figured Dan would be sitting very carefully for a while. And he deserved whatever his wife gave him. Trouble was, the bastard would probably enjoy it entirely too much. But that wasn't Simon's problem now. He had one thing on his mind, and that was finding Francie.

Chapter Sixteen

Finding Francie turned out to be blessedly easy.

'You came back.' Simon struggled to breathe around the sudden tightness in his chest at the sight of her.

'Of course I came back. I couldn't leave my plants, could I? No one here knows how to take care of them properly.' Francie was on her hands and knees sowing French beans, her sundress barely covering the lovely bottom he so adored. 'Now go away,' she said. 'I'm busy.'

'Then I'll help you. Work always goes faster with two.' He knelt next to her, shook a few beans from the packet into his hand and began to drop a couple in each of the holes she had meticulously dug with the dibber. It was the same dibber that had been converted so recently to such an exquisite sex toy.

'I don't want your help. Go away.'

'Not gonna happen,' he said taking the dibber away from her and grabbing her hands when she slapped at him. 'I'm not going anywhere until we settle this.'

She jerked away from him and stood up so fast she nearly toppled backward into the courgettes. 'If you won't go, then I'll leave, damn it.'

She had a helluva stride, but his legs were longer, and he was faster. He practically tackled her from behind, both of them stumbling against the brick wall. He threw an arm up to protect her from the abrasive impact, which bashed his elbow, taking off the skin, as he settled on to his forearm with her cradled between him and the wall. His other hand was splayed over the rapid rise and fall of her belly with just enough pressure to keep her from bolting. And, God, the feel of her there all warm and soft and spicy-sweet with the smell of her sweat and her sex and the outdoors they both loved, it was almost more than he could bear. It was as though everything in him pressed out through every pore, pressed out to get closer to her. 'Dan never paid me to be with you.' Simon forced the words up through his tight throat. 'He offered. I said no.'

She squirmed beneath him, but he held her tight. 'When I came to you that first time it wasn't my intention to … to have you like I did. I'd hoped that maybe I could win you some other way, that maybe I could help you realise

Dan couldn't give you what you wanted, but maybe someone else could.' He kissed her ear. 'Maybe I could.'

She squirmed again and her skirt rucked up between them, leaving only the thin fabric of her knickers separating her bare bottom from his fly. His cock responded with enthusiasm.

'Then I had you.' He spoke into her neck. 'And after we made love, I would have done anything to have you again, to be with you again. Because every time I was with you was one more chance to win you away from him. My being with you was completely mercenary, Francie. I didn't care about Dan or his suffering for you. I was there because I wanted you. If I had to endure Dan's presence to get to you, well so be it.'

She was trembling, shaking all over, and he realised she was crying quietly. He pulled her still closer until he heard her breath catch. 'I want it to be me in your life, Francie, me and not Dan. I'm sorry I hurt you. It was never what I wanted to do.'

He relaxed his arm around her waist. But she didn't move. She just stayed there in his embrace saying nothing, until the silence stretched tight and demanding. 'Francie?'

'Be quiet, Simon. Just shut up, OK?' She took the hand that rested on her belly and moved it up to slide inside the bodice of her dress against her breast, and her nipple hardened and pressed against his palm. 'I don't want any more words. I want you to make love to me. Just the two of us, this time. No one else.' Then she pushed her bottom back hard against his fly so that his erection pressed into the thinly clad valley between her arse cheeks, and he groaned at the delicious agony of it.

She reached around awkwardly to worry open his fly, but she let him finish the task with the hand not cupping and exploring inside her dress.

'Hurry,' she said. 'I need you.'

He shoved at his trousers and boxers until he could feel the cool evening air on his bare arse, then he released his cock against her bottom, raked aside the crotch of her panties and slid his hand down to stroke the swelling folds of her pussy. She caught her breath in little whimpers and pressed back hard against his hand, wetting his palm with her efforts, rubbing her heavy clit against his calloused fingers, pumping and shifting and filling the air with the urgent scent of her. 'I need you to fuck me, Simon. I need you now.' Her voice was little more than a harsh whisper.

Once again she reached behind her, slapping his hand away, grabbing his cock, then opening her stance and lifting one leg slightly, giving him a mouth-watering glimpse of her, all slippery and engorged. She moved, settled, then sheathed him deep in her tight grip.

'Oh God,' he cried out, burying his face against her nape and burrowing a hand into the front of her knickers to tweak and thumb her clit. It only took a few thrusts

169

before she came, flooding the insides of her thighs, gripping him so hard he could barely keep from coming himself. But it was too soon. He wasn't ready yet. This time it was just the two of them, and he wanted to make it last. He pulled out of her and she turned on him, pushing, shoving, manoeuvring until they were both down on the ground, in between the tidy rows of climbing peas, until he felt the warm earth against his arse. Then she slipped out of her panties. Holding the skirt of her dress wadded against her belly, she moved to straddle him. She squatted over his face, squatted so he could see her exquisite landscape, the blood-red gape of her aroused cunt, the pearled erection of her clit, the tight dark knot of her anus. She squatted still lower until her swollen labia just brushed his lips, and he strained his neck to nibble and kiss each in turn before she slid the wet splay of her down over his chest. She reached behind her to grasp his penis, then lifted her bottom and settled on to it with a sigh, a sigh he echoed. Her breasts were pressed up and out above the gaping front of her dress, and as they found their rhythm, he reached up to cup and caress, stroking her nipples to hard, heavy points above the tight sway and bounce of her.

Somewhere in their lovemaking she had lost her gardening clogs, and she curled her bare feet into the soft soil, pressing down hard against the earth for leverage, and God, what leverage it was!

'Francie,' he gasped 'I can't hold out much longer. I need to come.'

She leaned forward on his chest and kissed him hard. 'Then I want you on top,' she breathed.

He pulled her to him and rolled with her, her legs locking around his hips as he did so. Then, on his knees, he drove into her hard enough to make her gasp, hard enough to make her whimper, hard enough to make her growl out her orgasm. She clawed at him and shuddered until he could barely hold her, gripping his cock so tight in her spasming pussy that he lost the battle for control and came in deep convulsive waves that felt like they'd never stop. All the while, she covered his face with kisses and whispered his name.

* * *

'You're a worse voyeur than I am, Bel.' Dan came to the bedroom window where his wife stood, as naked as he was, peeking around the edge of the curtain into the walled garden. 'Are they all right?' He reached to caress her breast and she wriggled her bottom against his cock, which was already on the rise again.

'Very all right, I'd say. And they managed quite the romp without so much as damaging a single plant. Such is the sex life of consummate gardeners, I suppose.'

He peered around the curtain, sliding his hand down

171

over her belly to caress her very wet pussy. 'Looks like they're taking the fun inside. I can imagine they'd both need a shower to wash the soil off all their bits. Darling, are you crying?'

Bel gave a little sniff. 'Oh, I can't help it, Dan. They're such a lovely couple, aren't they? I was so worried they'd miss their chance at happiness.' She reached up and stroked his cheek tenderly. 'No one should miss their chance at happiness, Dan.'

'No, darling, they shouldn't. And now that the garden porn has finished for the evening, perhaps I can persuade you back to bed for another ride on my very needy cock.' He gave his growing erection a stroke and thrust his hips playfully in her direction.

She fingered her pussy absently, still looking out of the window, pretending she didn't notice his cock. But he knew she did, and if she didn't he was pretty sure he could find ways of getting her attention.

'I'm really rather hungry, darling.' She sighed and gave a huge stretch, forcing her lovely breasts forward. 'But I suppose I could manage one more go before I'm too famished to fuck.'

She lay back on the rumpled bed, opened her legs and wriggled her bottom. 'I'll even let you ride me from the top, darling, since I can only imagine how sore your lovely pink arse is.' She nodded towards the suede belt still draped threateningly over the headboard.

'But I'm warning you, I might not be so lenient next time.'

Before he pushed into her, he gave her a long lingering kiss and cupped her flushed face in his hand. 'Then I'll be very careful to make sure there is no next time, unless of course it's a joint effort.'

She chuckled wickedly. 'You don't suppose Francie and Simon would be interested in a little –'

He stopped her words with another kiss and began to thrust playfully. 'I think that might be a bridge too far for the moment, darling, but in the future possibly. Just possibly.' Then, in spite of his tender, stinging buttocks, he rolled with her so that she straddled him and he could play with her lovely breasts and see the pleasure on her face while he made love to his beautiful, nasty wife.

The End

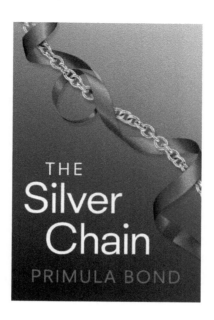

THE SILVER CHAIN – PRIMULA BOND

Good things come to those who wait…

After a chance meeting one evening, mysterious entrepreneur Gustav Levi and photographer Serena Folkes agree to a very special contract.

Gustav will launch Serena's photographic career at his gallery, but only if Serena agrees to become his companion.

To mark their agreement, Gustav gives Serena a bracelet and silver chain which binds them physically and symbolically. A sign that Serena is under Gustav's power.

As their passionate relationship intensifies, the silver chain pulls them closer together. But will Gustav's past tear them apart?

A passionate, unforgettable erotic romance for fans of *50 Shades of Grey* and Sylvia Day's *Crossfire Trilogy*.

GAME – JUSTINE ELYOT

The stakes are high, the game is on.

In this sequel to Justine Elyot's bestselling *On Demand*, Sophie discovers a whole new world of daring sexual exploits.

Sophie's sexual tastes have always been a bit on the wild side – something her boyfriend Lloyd has always loved about her.

But Sophie gives Lloyd every part of her body except her heart. To win all of her, Lloyd challenges Sophie to live out her secret fantasies.

As the game intensifies, she experiments with all kinds of kinks and fetishes in a bid to understand what she really wants. But Lloyd feature in her final decision? Or will the ultimate risk he takes drive her away from him?

Find out more at www.mischiefbooks.com

POWER PLAY – CHARLOTTE STEIN

Now she's the boss, everything that once seemed forbidden is possible…

Meet Eleanor Harding, a woman who loves to be in control and who puts Anastasia Steele in the shade.

When Eleanor is promoted, she loses two very important things: the heated relationship she had with her boss, and control over her own desires.

She finds herself suddenly craving something very different – and office junior, Ben, seems like just the sort of man to fulfil her needs. He's willing to show her all of the things she's been missing – namely, what it's like to be the one in charge.

Now all Eleanor has to do is decide…is Ben calling the kinky shots, or is she?

Find out more at www.mischiefbooks.com

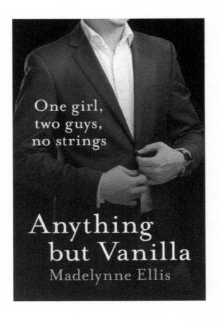

ANYTHING BUT VANILLA
MADELYNNE ELLIS

One girl, two guys, no strings.

Kara North is on the run. Fleeing from her controlling fiancé and a wedding she never wanted, she accepts the chance offer of refuge on Liddell Island, where she soon catches the eye of the island's owner, erotic photographer Ric Liddell.

But pleasure comes in more than one flavour when Zachary Blackwater, the charming ice-cream vendor also takes an interest, and wants more than just a tumble in the sun.

When Kara learns that the two men have been unlikely lovers for years, she becomes obsessed with the idea of a threesome.

Soon Kara is wondering how she ever considered committing herself to just one man.

Find out more at www.mischiefbooks.com

Lightning Source UK Ltd.
Milton Keynes UK
UKHW011336041119
352868UK00008B/595/P

9 780007 534760